THE PAYBACK

PREVIOUS BOOKS BY ALAN REFKIN

FICTION

Matt Moretti and Han Li Series

The Archivist
The Abductions

Mauro Bruno Detective Series

The Patriarch
The Scion
The Artifact

NONFICTION

The Wild, Wild East: Lessons for Success in Business in Contemporary Capitalist China
Alan Refkin and Daniel Borgia, PhD

Doing the China Tango: How to Dance around Common Pitfalls in Chinese Business Relationships
Alan Refkin and Scott Cray

Conducting Business in the Land of the Dragon: What Every Businessperson Needs to Know about China
Alan Refkin and Scott Cray

Piercing the Great Wall of Corporate China: How to Perform Forensic Due Diligence on Chinese Companies
Alan Refkin and David Dodge

THE PAYBACK

A MATT MORETTI AND HAN LI THRILLER

ALAN REFKIN

THE PAYBACK
A MATT MORETTI AND HAN LI THRILLER

iUniverse books may be ordered through booksellers or by contacting:

iUniverse
1663 Liberty Drive
Bloomington, IN 47403
www.iuniverse.com
1-800-Authors (1-800-288-4677)

ISBN: 978-1-6632-0180-5 (sc)
ISBN: 978-1-6632-0181-2 (e)

Library of Congress Control Number: 2020909442

Print information available on the last page.

iUniverse rev. date: 06/05/2020

To my wife, Kerry, my best friend and
compass in our journey through life

To Carol Ogden Jones

PROLOGUE

Grozny, the Soviet Union
December 15, 1991

Winter came early this year, and it was cold—not a nip in the air and put-on-a-sweater crispness but a bone-chilling frigidness. It was just past midnight when Major General Vitaly Barinov grabbed the bottle of Green Label vodka from inside his overcoat and took a healthy swig. He told himself it was to keep warm, but that was a lie. He was an alcoholic, and although vodka was his beverage of choice, in a pinch any form of alcohol would do. He looked at his watch and saw that Kasym was twenty minutes late and counting. He cursed this tardiness and the fact that he was freezing his ass off waiting for him. Because Barinov had Raynaud's disease, which meant that the blood vessels in his extremities spasmed and contracted in extremely cold temperatures, his fingers and toes became so numb in the cold that he could barely feel them.

Barinov removed a pack of cigarettes and a lighter from his coat pocket and lit one of the unfiltered cancer sticks. He inhaled the smoke deep into his lungs, coughed several times when the organs protested the combination of cold weather and smoke, then took a second pull with the same results. He couldn't wait to leave Grozny and return to Moscow, although it wasn't any warmer there. But at least he could get a decent meal and better vodka. All he needed was for Abdul-Malik Kasym, who'd been his nuclear weapons maintenance technician these past two years and who was in contact with a buyer, to provide proof that the money promised to Barinov had been posted to his offshore bank account. Once this was verified, he'd give Kasym the merchandise for his buyer and hop on a military flight to Moscow. There he'd see a friend in the government, obtain a new identity, and disappear to someplace warm. He'd sacrificed enough for the homeland during his thirty-year military career—two wives, three children who barely knew him, and a couple of holes in his right leg that caused a slight limp, compliments of his second tour of duty in Afghanistan.

The world knew that the seemingly invincible Soviet Union had imploded and would dissolve in eleven days to become fifteen independent nations. What frightened Soviet officials, as well as the new leadership that would take control, was not the political transition. It was the fact that the Soviet Ministry of Defense had dispersed 22,000 tactical nuclear weapons into areas such as Grozny and had yet to repatriate all of them to Moscow, where they could be better safeguarded. Now, with the USSR coming apart at the seams more rapidly than anticipated, the ministry's previous timetable for completing this consolidation of nuclear weapons in the next eleven days had been thrown out the window. Every transport plane that could get into the air had a team on board that had been ordered to quickly get back the remaining thermonuclear devices before they were stolen and sold in the chaos that was accompanying this transition of power.

There was ample concern that some of these weapons might turn up missing because the slogan throughout the country, especially the farther from Moscow one went, was that everything was for sale. With corruption rampant and inflation approaching two thousand percent, everything indeed was. Barinov, like most other government employees, pensioners, and workers, hadn't been paid in months. And there was no indication from the incoming president of when or if they ever would be. That tardiness in wage and pension payments doubled and tripled to nonmilitary in the outlying regions of the Soviet Union. Therefore, what choice did anyone have? In the minds of many, selling stolen goods wasn't about theft; it was about survival.

Barinov took another swig of vodka, this one a little longer than the last, and returned the bottle back inside his overcoat. Stomping his boots hard on the concrete pavement and clapping his hands together in a failed attempt to get more blood flowing into his limbs, he again cursed Kasym for being late.

He took a last hit off his cigarette, coughed, and was about to light another when he saw Kasym slowly walking toward him. "You're late," he gruffly said.

"A thousand apologizes. I just finished speaking to my buyer, and the call lasted longer than I anticipated."

"We haven't much time. Cargo planes and troops will arrive in a few hours to pick up the nuclear weapons. That gives you very little time to get them out of the bunkers and off the base."

"Do you have the necessary documents?"

"You're authorized to remove two milling machines, a spare-parts container, and a truck from the base. The guards will think you're stealing the machinery even with my authorization, but if you give them a few US dollars they won't open the crates or argue about the truck leaving the base. I've put all the ancillary parts that I could find for this type of weapon in the spare-parts container and had it placed in one of the bunkers. Call it my parting gift to you."

"Thank you. I hadn't considered asking for the spare parts. You're sure that the guards outside the bunkers will let us remove the weapons?"

"I'm in charge of the nuclear arsenal, so they'll obey my orders."

"And the records on these weapons?"

"Erased from computer inventories in both Moscow and Grozny, as per our agreement—which brings us to my money. Do you have the confirmation of the wire transfer?"

"No," Kasym said, without a trace of emotion in his voice. "The buyer told me not to pay you."

"We had a deal for twenty million US dollars. How much is your client willing to pay?"

"Nothing," Kasym said, removing a Makarov PB with suppressor from his left inside coat pocket and pointing it at Barinov. "I'm taking the weapons, and you're retiring early."

Barinov quickly turned around as his brain gave the command to his lower extremities to run. But with a total lack of feeling in both limbs, he didn't go anywhere. Instead he fell hard on his face, breaking both his nose and the bottle of vodka in his pocket. Turning over on his back, he saw Kasym walk toward him and lower his weapon so that it pointed at the center of his face. Before his brain could process any more information, two bullets entered his cerebrum and blew a half-dollar-sized hole out the back of his skull.

CHAPTER 1

Present day

THE TOWN OF Miramshah lay in North Waziristan, a rugged, mountainous area of northwest Pakistan where outsiders were looked upon with suspicion and were encouraged, by whatever means necessary, to leave. Located a little over ten miles from the Pakistan-Afghanistan border, until recently the town had been widely known as a secure hiding place for the leadership of various terror groups seeking refuge from governments that were bent on killing them. Except for the occasional CIA drone strike, Miramshah had long been nearly devoid of wholesale violence. One reason for this was that the jihadists residing there tended to leave each other alone, choosing instead to kill foreigners and outsiders of differing religious beliefs. Another reason for the area's tranquility was that the Pakistani army didn't bother the town, considering its residents to be good militants, "good" being a term the army used to describe terrorists who didn't kill Pakistanis.

One of the good militant groups recognized by the Pakistani government was the Protectors of Islam, whose core philosophy was that foreigners must leave the Middle East and Africa or die. The United States, unsurprisingly, had an opposing point of view. Therefore, it had periodically carried out drone attacks in North Waziristan to prune the group's leadership tree. Although this angered the government of Pakistan, there was little it could do to stop these airstrikes. However, these past attacks had had a marginal effect on the terrorist group because the Protectors was ruled by one man, Awalmir Afridi, who alone called the shots. Mid- and upper-level members were there only to pass along his instructions, to assist members with executing his orders, and to keep complainers in line—which usually meant killing them. As a result, if someone below Afridi was killed, that person was quickly replaced by another non-decision-making functionary who was just as ambitious and eager to carry out the leader's orders as the person he replaced.

Over the years, an unofficial understanding between the United States and the Protectors of Islam had gradually materialized, with the United States not putting boots on the ground to go after Afridi or increasing its airstrikes as long as the terrorist leader kept his jihad in the Middle East and Africa and off American soil. There was no written agreement to this effect or meeting between parties to verbally acknowledge this—it had just become the way it was.

This fragile equilibrium had remained in place until three months ago, when the presidents of the United States and China, along with four senior Chinese officials, were abducted by individuals who claimed to be members of the Protectors of Islam. Shortly afterward, both countries had been informed that they had seventy-two hours to meet the demands given in a video, which showed the hostages kneeling before a Protectors flag, or the hostages would be killed. As the deadline approached, the kidnappers thought that they'd make their seriousness clear. They beheaded the four Chinese officials and posted the grisly killings on the internet. They were saving the execution of both presidents until the following day in the event their demands weren't met. Afridi, who didn't have computer or cell service at his home, didn't know about any of this. He learned of the kidnappings and the fact that they'd been attributed to his terrorist group only when one of his advisors journeyed to his home and told him what had happened.

The day after the Chinese officials were killed, with virtually the entire world watching live on the internet, the two heads of state had knelt in front of two balaclava-clad men, each of whom held a knife tightly to the throat of the president before him. Behind them was the flag of the Protectors of Islam. However, at exactly 6:00 p.m., the time of the scheduled executions, the video feed ended. At that point, the entire world believed that the presidents had been beheaded and that the Chinese and American governments had somehow interrupted the internet feed to prevent their executions from being seen. The real cause of the outage, however, was that Matt Moretti, a former Army Ranger, and Han Li, China's premier assassin, destroyed the equipment providing the feed and rescued the two presidents a moment before their executioners could separate their heads from their bodies. The problem was that the entire world believed the two presidents were dead. Therefore, the acting presidents of China and the United States had launched over two hundred cruise missiles at Protectors of Islam strongholds throughout the Middle East and Africa. Within a matter of minutes, the once-large terrorist group had been decimated, although Afridi survived the bombardment by hiding within a family cave in the nearby mountains.

Framing a terrorist group with an act of terror wasn't hard. Metaphorically, it was like falling off a log. In this case, the kidnappers had only had to display the group's flag behind the hostages and claim to be members of the Protectors of Islam. Afridi's denial of his group's involvement, which he never made, would have been meaningless given his reputation and the fact that his flag was displayed behind the hostages and viewed on the internet by well over a billion people.

Now, three months after the beheadings, the terrorist leader had switched his focus from setting the record straight to getting revenge against the perpetrators of this hoax. He viewed two organizations as the probable culprits behind this charade—the CIA and China's Ministry of State Security, the MSS. Both had the sophistication and resources to abduct two of the most heavily guarded people in the world and expertly frame Afridi for it. In addition, both nations had pulverized his encampments and followers with two hundred cruise missiles. Left with nothing but the clothes on his back, he vowed to pay back both countries in a way that would hurt them for generations and make 9/11 look like amateur hour.

Prince Husam Al Hakim was running late. He quickly put the documents he had been examining back into the large accordion folder and returned the folder to his safe. He wanted to be sure of his facts before a meeting in Peshawar, Pakistan, with someone he'd assumed was dead. Since he was a Saudi royal, the Shaheen Air flight would probably wait for him, but that was a roll of the dice since he wasn't exactly at the top of the House of Saud's food chain. He was somewhere in the middle of the 2,000-member inner circle of the royal family. He was, however, in the top 10 percent if one considered there were 20,000 royals. The even more distant relatives received, on average, a paltry few thousand dollars a month from the kingdom in acknowledgment of the few drops of royal blood coursing through their veins, versus the $100,000 stipend he was given because he had more royal hemoglobin within him.

Al Hakim was worth slightly over $5 billion. He made his money by acting as a middleman in the illicit sale of arms to Middle Eastern and African governments that were fighting terrorism and by investing in oil futures, where the inside information he gleaned from other family members gave him a predictive edge. He had no position within the government, nor was he ever asked for his opinion by the king or any relatives who occupied bureaucratic positions. The reason for this was simple—they knew that he didn't agree with many government policies, especially those that were conciliatory toward the West. Nevertheless, he publicly supported the king's policies because any public disagreement with the monarchy would get his stipend reduced to the wages of a fast-food employee or else result in his incarceration until the king decided he'd extracted his pound of flesh.

However, the real reason that he disagreed with most of the other family members regarding their deference to the West was that he needed a continuing conflict in the region in order to make money. He couldn't sell arms and bullets if no one was shooting at each other. It was also difficult to make money in oil futures without price movement, which was usually caused by the unpredictable outcome of outside events. That was why he'd long ago taken out an insurance policy in the form of bankrolling the Protectors of Islam to create chaos in the region. That partnership had worked well, creating profits in both his enterprises. However, when the United States and China decided to pulverize the Protectors by launching two hundred cruise missiles at its Middle Eastern and African strongholds, his insurance policy had ended abruptly—or so Al Hakim had believed.

The Bacha Khan International Airport was a ten-minute drive from the business district of Peshawar, Pakistan. By international standards the airport was small, with just over a million passengers passing through its four terminals per year. It did, however, have something that didn't exist at any other airport in the world, in that its single 9,000-foot-long, 150-foot-wide runway was crossed by an aging railway line. Apparently, those who had built the landing strip thought that ground and air travel could peacefully coexist and that the two modes of transportation would work out the scheduling between them to avoid conflict. Most pilots discounted this notion of synchronous harmony, especially in Pakistan, where coordination between parties was considered a matter of perspective. Pilots therefore maintained a razor-sharp situational awareness on both takeoffs and landings, praying they wouldn't see a locomotive crossing in front of them. But as unique as a rail line was, the airport was better known for what had occurred there in the 1960s, when U-2 pilot Francis Gary Powers took off from Bacha Khan and was later shot down and captured by the Soviet Union. Half a century later, Husam Al Hakim's flight would uneventfully set down on that same runway.

Al Hakim was traditionally dressed, in a white dishdasha— an ankle-length garment resembling a robe—and a keffiyeh, which was a square of fabric folded into a triangle, held in place by a circlet of camel hair, and placed on the head so that a point was directed to each shoulder and down the back. Once he'd cleared customs and immigration and entered the baggage claim area, dozens of men energetically approached, all trying to get him to use their car service or take advantage of the adult entertainment that they were willing to arrange. Al Hakim dismissed each solicitation with a flick of his hand or a stern look. As the group around him thinned, he saw a six foot two man who appeared to be in his late thirties or early forties, with a full black beard and wearing a light gray *shalwar kameez*, a two-piece garment consisting of pantaloons and a tunic. He was standing against the back wall, holding a sign with no name on it—the sign that Al Hakim had been told to expect. This must be Jabir Samara, Awalmir Afridi's cousin.

"Kayf Haalak?" Samara asked as Al Hakim approached him.

"Bi-khayr, al-Hamdu lillah," Al Hakim responded, indicating that he was well and that he praised God for it.

Once the correct question and answer had been exchanged, Samara silently led the way to an aging, dusty white Toyota Corolla, which had more than its fair share of dents and scrapes on its rusted exterior.

"How far are we going?" Al Hakim asked as they drove away from the airport. "My return flight leaves in three hours."

"My cousin is ten minutes away. Once your meeting is over, I'll drive you back."

Satisfied, Al Hakim leaned back in the torn black fabric seat.

Exactly nine minutes after they left the airport, the paved highway they were on turned sharply to the left. Instead of remaining on it, Samara veered the vehicle to the right and onto a narrow dirt strip. On both sides of the Toyota, as far as Al Hakim could see, the landscape consisted of tumbleweeds interspersed with rocks and boulders, all scattered haphazardly across the brown earth.

Two minutes after they diverted onto the dirt strip, they pulled in front of a weatherworn brown-brick structure measuring twenty feet to a side, with a roof that resembled a quilt of sorts because of the colored metal patches spread across it. No other structure was visible in any direction. Al Hakim got out of the car, stretched, and followed Afridi's cousin inside.

The interior of the dwelling had no partitions. A metal cot with an oil lamp beside it sat in one corner, and in the center of the room was a small rusted table that at one time had been black, along with four matching chairs in similar condition. On top of the table was a propane burner heating a pot of water and two nondescript tea glasses.

"It's good to see you again, old friend," Afridi said, stepping forward to greet the Saudi prince.

"And you as well."

They exchanged an air kiss to each other's right cheek, followed by the left. Afridi then pointed to one of the rusted chairs at the table, before sitting in the adjoining chair to the left. While Samara took over the duties of preparing their tea, Afridi brought Al Hakim up-to-date on what had occurred following his alleged kidnapping of the presidents. He told the story of how he had hidden in a cave not far from his home in North Waziristan and had nearly been buried alive by the massive American cruise missile attack. During a pause in the conversation, Samara handed each of the men their Maghrebi mint tea and then went outside.

"Does your cousin live in Peshawar?" Al Hakim asked before taking a sip of the tea.

"He owns a fig and date farm in Bannu, which is a three-hour drive from here. His wife and children were killed when an American cruise missile destroyed one of my strongholds, where they were spending the night while on their way to visit relatives."

Al Hakim nodded. "You indicated in your message that you had urgent business to discuss. What could be important enough for you to abandon the cover of death that the Americans have gifted you?"

Afridi slowly set his tea down on the table. "I intend to detonate two nuclear weapons inside China—the ones you once told me you had in your possession. You do still have them?"

Stunned by what he'd just heard, Al Hakim took a moment to respond. "I'm an arms dealer, and I sell weapons for profit. I have them, and I pay quite a sum of money to ensure they're in good condition because their value on the black market appreciates every year. They're worth a fortune. When their value plateaus, I'll anonymously sell them to the United States, which will gladly pay substantially more than market value to keep them out of the hands of terrorists such as yourself."

"You'll make more if you give them to me to detonate."

"You'll have to explain the economics of that to me, because the value of these weapons after detonation is zero."

Afridi explained that following the explosions in two major cities and the subsequent radiological fallout, China would be economically devastated and need huge amounts of cash to begin a long and expensive reconstruction process. This would require dipping into its cash reserves, which would be insufficient to cover the costs associated with this catastrophe. Therefore, China would be forced to sell the

$1.2 trillion of US Treasury notes that it currently held. As these were liquidated or matured and new Treasuries weren't purchased to replace them, interest rates in the United States would increase, and the national debt would skyrocket.

"Economics 101. But how would I make money? Because setting off nuclear devices doesn't equate to an increase in arms sales since the United States and China produce arms and don't purchase them from people such as myself."

"My plan will give you far more than the paltry amount of money you can generate from selling weapons. You'll be making money at the sovereign state level."

"Explain."

"I assume that the series of dummy companies that you set up to funnel money to me can be modified to show that the king is the one who sent me funds over the years?"

"I can change the documentation relating to the ownership of any one of my shell companies at any time. Why?"

"Because just before the detonations, when it's too late to prevent the explosions, you'll warn the Chinese and give them documentation that proves the king funded my organization over the years, which gave me the money to purchase nuclear weapons. That documentation will include your offshore bank statements, which will be in the shell company's name, showing the wiring of money to me. I'll provide you with my documentation for receipt of the funds and a private handwritten letter to the king expressing my gratitude for his assistance in moving the weapons onto Chinese soil."

"The obvious question the Chinese will have is why the king of Saudi Arabia would be helping you," said Al Hakim. "That makes no sense because our country will also be hurt, since we have investments in China and the United States.

And you've been quoted numerous times as saying that you want to remove the king from the throne."

"You know as well as I that many in the royal family fund terrorist organizations. They either believe in the cause or give them money because they're scared these organizations will start focusing on Saudi Arabia and incite the people against the monarchy."

"That's true," Al Hakim confessed.

"Given the threat of my organization, governments won't think that this backdoor funding is unusual. They'll believe that the king's actions were predicated on the belief that paying me kept my followers from coming into the kingdom and inciting the people to remove him from power. They'll also believe that the king doesn't care about destroying a country that prefers to buy oil from Russia and Iran."

"You realize that everyone will know you're alive once I hand over the documentation and that the Chinese, the Americans, and others will come after you?"

"Giving up my anonymity is unfortunately necessary to get my payback and regain the confidence of my followers. Take this," Afridi said, lifting a thick manila folder off the floor beside his chair and handing it to Al Hakim. "This is the documentation and letter that I mentioned. Tell the Chinese you saw this on the king's desk when he asked you to get something from his office. If you don't like that explanation, then make up another. Either way, you stumbled upon this information and copied it. Any Western intelligence agency can authenticate my signature."

"Let me ask you again—how do I make money? You mentioned something about the sovereign state level?"

Afridi took a sip of tea and then explained that the Chinese wouldn't take the destruction of two of their cities

11

lying down. "There is little doubt," Afridi said, "that they will force the Saudi king off the throne either by a threat of force or by sending troops into the country to take over the government. However, the Chinese can't annex Saudi Arabia under their flag or be an occupying force for long, because the Saudi people won't accept a foreign country ruling them. In addition, the rest of the world will also unite against this because no one wants the Chinese to control a significant portion of the world's oil."

Al Hakim said that he agreed with that assumption.

"That's where you come in. The Chinese will trust you because you turned against your king to try to protect them. They'll need someone on the throne who's friendly to their interests and whom they trust. You're the only person who will satisfy both requirements. If they don't approach you with this offer, suggest it to them. They'll have no other choice. The documentation that you gave them will validate your credibility and desire to protect Chinese interests."

"The king will refuse to give up the throne. After all, he will know the accusations against him are false."

"The Chinese won't give him a choice, and they'll have the moral high ground in the opinion of the world, given the documentation we will have provided."

"So in your scenario, I make money because I'm the king."

"Since you'll be handing out the royal allowances, the entire family will be sucking up to you. Those that don't will eventually come around once they realize that it's either you or the Chinese who will rule over Saudi Arabia. I only ask that you give me a secure hiding place in the kingdom, known only to you and me, where I'll live on a generous dowry that you'll provide. After facial reconstructive surgery, no one will recognize me."

Al Hakim leaned back in his chair and took a sip of tea, after which he gently set the cup down on the table. "Make your preparations, and I'll get my documentation in order when I return to Riyadh. We'll continue to use the one-time pads to communicate over email, just as we did for this meeting. An OTP is unbreakable, even by the NSA."

"Are you sure of that?"

"The random key we use to encrypt and decrypt our communication exists only between us and is destroyed after use. That makes our code unbreakable."

Afridi acknowledged that since they hadn't been attacked by a drone after setting up this meeting over the internet, the OTP seemed to operate as advertised.

"God willing," Al Hakim said as he took the manila folder and stood, "the next time we see each other, I'll be on the throne."

"Inshallah," Afridi replied.

Ahmed al-Khobar was a private detective. He was twenty-seven years of age, five nine, and thin, and he had the whitest teeth that money could buy. He considered himself lucky with women in a country that repressed sexual urges. He'd also had more than a few dalliances with married women that easily could have cost him his head in the public square. Besides a strong desire to find out what was under the head-to-toe clothing worn by women, his other passion was driving fast cars. Perhaps that was why he got along so well with his boss. His employer, the Saudi Arabian minister of the interior, Prince Mahamat bin Salman, knew al-Khobar's weaknesses and took advantage of them, rewarding him with what he wanted most when he performed well. The detective had use of the prince's $320,000 Ferrari F12 Berlinetta, and just as importantly, his royal plates meant that he could park wherever and go as fast as he dared without fear of reprisal.

The assignment the prince had given him was somewhat unusual, in that it had required him follow a member of the royal family to Peshawar—not his favorite place on Earth. He hadn't been told why he was following this person, but the good news was that he was returning to Riyadh that evening on the same flight as the royal. For this assignment al-Khobar was disguised as a low-level businessman. He wore a cheap suit, scuffed shoes, and an out-of-style tie. He considered this the perfect disguise because royals rarely paid attention to those of a lower social status, especially those who flew in economy.

Upon arriving at Peshawar, he followed Husam Al Hakim into the international arrival terminal. Avoiding the horde of drivers seeking his business, he saw the royal walk up to a driver who was holding a blank sign. The man seemed to be expecting Al Hakim because there was little conversation and, most significantly, no haggling over the price of services. Al-Khobar watched as they left the terminal and got into an aging Toyota Corolla. Just after they drove off, he grabbed one of the drivers who was milling around, quickly settled on a price, and got into the man's Volkswagen Golf. He could see the Toyota nearly half a mile ahead, and he directed the driver to keep pace with it and not close the gap. The driver followed the Toyota onto a dirt road, and when the vehicle stopped in front of the only structure within sight, al-Khobar told the driver to pull over and stop. Grabbing the backpack that he'd brought with him, which contained his camera and a few odds and ends, he jumped out of the car. Pushing a wad of cash into the driver's hand, he told him to turn around and go back to the main road and wait for him there.

The detective sprinted into the brush and set off at a quick jog parallel to the dirt road. He ran around the tumbleweeds and boulders for nearly fifteen minutes until, winded and gasping for air, he stood behind an outcropping of brush a hundred yards from the decaying structure in front of which the Toyota was parked. A few minutes later, Al Hakim's driver exited the structure and began chain-smoking cigarettes beside his vehicle. Al-Khobar took photos of the driver and the building, then waited for half an hour until the front door opened and two men walked outside. One was the royal he was following; the other, he recognized as Awalmir Afridi, who everyone on the planet thought was dead. His heart began to race as he switched from photo to video, zoomed in as much as he could, and began recording. Normally, he sent his photos and video to his employer via his camera's built-in Wi-Fi or his cell phone, to provide a heads-up before he spoke with him or filed his report. However, when he checked his devices, he saw that he had no internet or cellular reception, so he'd have to defer sending the information until he could get a signal.

He'd just slung his camera over his shoulder and was about to head back to the main highway to catch his ride back to the airport when a large shadow appeared in front of him. Turning around, he faced a bearded man, six feet, two inches in height, who deftly pulled a long knife from under his left sleeve and arched it across al-Khobar's throat, slicing it from ear to ear. Unable to speak or breathe, the detective collapsed to the ground, dying within seconds.

Samara frisked the man, who was staring at the sky with a perpetual expression of shock and surprise, careful to avoid the blood that had pooled around the body. After removing a passport, wallet, cash, and airline ticket from the dead man's pockets, he unslung the camera off the man's shoulder and walked back to the Toyota Corolla, where Afridi and Al Hakim stood waiting for him.

"Just one person?" Afridi asked.

"Just one. Either he parked his car some distance away, or someone dropped him off. I'll see if I pick up a tail when I return to the airport."

"It's fortunate that you saw the light reflecting off his camera."

"Fortunate for us, fatal for him. This is what he had on him," Samara said, handing over the man's belongings.

"Let's see what we have," Afridi said, opening the passport and seeing that the dead man was a Yemeni by the name of Ahmed al-Khobar. He then looked at the boarding pass that had been issued to him in Riyadh and his return ticket.

"Do you recognize this man?" Afridi asked Al Hakim, handing him al-Khobar's passport.

"No."

Afridi and Al Hakim then looked at the photos and video recorded on the camera.

"Someone had him following you," Afridi said. "I think we should accelerate our plans."

Al Hakim said that he agreed.

Afridi looked up at Samara. "Put the man's body in the trunk of your car and bury it where no one will find him," he said. "After that, make sure that you destroy the camera's memory chip and throw the camera in the hole with him."

Samara said that he understood. While Afridi and Al Hakim waited, Samara retrieved al-Khobar's body and threw it in the trunk of the Corolla. He then got into the vehicle and Al Hakim followed. As the Corolla kicked up a cloud of dust and pulled away from the weatherworn structure, Afridi went back inside.

When the Toyota entered the airport, al-Khobar's camera came to life, unbeknownst to the two men seated in the front of the car, having sensed and locked onto an internet signal. Had one of the men looked at the back seat, he would have seen a red light on the front of the camera indicating that it was transmitting whatever contents it held on its SanDisk memory card. The light was on for a total of three minutes and forty seconds, after which it went out. Had Samara been familiar with this airport, he also would have known what the locals already did—that the police Wi-Fi system encompassed the entire area of the Bacha Khan International Airport and could be utilized by anyone because there was no log-on. For that they could thank the chief of the airport police, who'd been at his job for thirty years and was anything but tech-savvy. Therefore, not wanting to appear stupid, he had ordered those setting up the police Wi-Fi system to eliminate security protocols so that any device he had in his hand could seamlessly find an internet connection.

By the time Samara pulled up to the terminal to drop off his passenger, al-Khobar's videos and photographs had already been received by Prince Mahamat bin Salman, Saudi Arabia's minister of the interior and overseer of the country's security.

CHAPTER 2

THE HATRED HAD officially started on February 23, 1944, when Stalin forcibly rounded up half a million Chechens from their homes, accusing them of collaborating with the Nazis. The paranoid Soviet leader, deeply suspicious of this ethnic Muslim group within his country's borders, ordered that they be herded onto cattle cars and sent to Western Siberia. More than half perished during the journey, and many more died in the harsh Siberian winter when they were abandoned in open fields and told to fend for themselves. This exile of the Chechen community within the borders of the Soviet Union continued until 1957, when Nikita Khrushchev extended an olive branch and permitted the Siberian Chechens to return home. But by that time, the damage had been done. With surprising uniformity, Chechens hated the Soviet Union and felt no allegiance to it. Then, in 1991, rumors began to circulate that the government was once again going to deport them to Siberia. The rumors had no basis in fact, but that didn't matter. Enough was enough. Banding together, the Chechen community resolved that they were going to fight rather than be exiled. Overthrowing the local government, they elected one of their own as president. Although this greatly pleased the Chechen people, it infuriated the Kremlin. Flatly stating that it would not grant independence and allow a separate Chechen state, Moscow sent in the military, fearful that if one region of the country wanted its own government, so would another.

Soviet hostility with the separatists continued through the dissolution of the Soviet Union and the formation of the Russian Federation. Over 80,000 Chechens and 4,000 Russian soldiers died during this conflict. However, if the Chechens thought they would eventually wear the Kremlin down and gain their freedom from the yoke of Russian rule, they were mistaken. During this time a virtually unknown prime minister named Vladimir Putin gained prominence, in no small part because of his harsh response to the separatist movement. The Chechen Republic's capital of Grozny was demolished to such an extent that the United Nations declared it the most destroyed city on Earth. The Chechens never forgot or forgave the Russians for exiling their parents or then crushing their bid for independence. In their minds Chechnya would always be independent, and they would never consider themselves Russian. Therefore, as a community, they covertly and sometimes openly resisted the Kremlin.

Abdul-Malik Kasym, a fourth-generation Chechen, had not been an active participant in the Chechen resistance decades ago. Instead, he had been considered a pacifist by all who knew him because of his unwillingness to become involved with covert activities against the Russians or even to demonstrate against them. This moniker of "pacifist" later had been changed to "traitor" when he got a job on the Russian military base in Grozny.

The day he announced his employment, every member of his family had shunned him. After he was branded a traitor within the community, no Chechen father would let his daughter date, much less marry, Kasym. Therefore, with no other options and wanting a family, Kasym had married a Russian cook who worked on the military base. The woman wasn't beautiful, but she gave him two strong sons, both of whom were then killed in the separatist wars of 1995. Kasym's wife died the following year, with some saying it was by her own hand while others said she was a casualty of the war.

Unknown to everyone, however, Abdul-Malik Kasym had always hated the Russians who occupied his ancestral land and considered himself a Chechen patriot. It had been evident to him that a resistance movement, no matter how well organized, wasn't going to force the Russians from Chechnya because of his homeland's strategic location and rich oil deposits. Instead, Kasym had concluded that if they weren't going to leave, then he'd try to impair their effectiveness. To accomplish this, he had decided to use the viral approach, meaning that just like a virus, he'd infect the host and attack from the inside.

Thus, once he had started working on the base, he had volunteered for the jobs no one else wanted, gained technical expertise in those positions from on-the-job training, and finally ended up in the least desirable position—nuclear weapons maintenance specialist. The two individuals who held this job worked long hours because of the age and number of weapons they were maintaining, and by regulation neither could drink alcohol or take drugs, substances for which they were routinely and frequently tested. These last two requisites made this an especially unpopular position for non-Chechen Russians, who probably had been given their first vodka in a baby bottle and used drugs to try to forget that they were assigned to the most destroyed city on Earth. Therefore, two highly trusted Chechens, who didn't drink or do drugs as a matter of religion, were routinely trained and certified for this type of maintenance. With virtually no days off and called at all hours in response to maintenance alarms, the average tech lasted six months to a year. Kasym was the exception: he kept the position for two years.

Over those two years, Kasym caused millions of dollars in damage by deftly sabotaging expensive equipment and erasing critical data from the base computer system. His focus widened, however, once the imam of his mosque introduced him to a Saudi prince, who had been referred to the imam by a religious leader in Riyadh. The prince had handed the imam an envelope containing a large sum of money and asked if the imam knew one of the people who maintained the military base's nuclear weapons and if that person might be willing to accept a consulting job with the prince's company. The imam was not an idiot. He knew that virtually everything in Russia and its satellite countries was being sold as the Soviet Union disintegrated, which was the reason the Saudi had come to Grozny. Therefore, the imam disclosed that he knew of one such person, and after a larger donation was negotiated, he set up a meeting between Kasym and Al Hakim.

Al Hakim's weapons provider in Grozny was the base commander, General Vitaly Barinov, who'd been on Al Hakim's payroll for years. The relationship between the two men was good, but Al Hakim knew that the general drank and fooled around too much to be trusted with keeping his mouth shut in the long run—which was the other reason he needed Kasym, in addition to needing the Chechen's ability to maintain the nuclear weapons that he was about to steal.

Kasym listened intently to what the Saudi proposed and accepted his offer of employment the very evening they met, indicating that he had no issue helping Al Hakim steal and then maintain nuclear weapons so long as they weren't detonated in Kasym's homeland and the Russians would be blamed for what happened. Once those assurances were made, they put together their plan. The next day, Kasym approached Barinov with an offer from an anonymous buyer to purchase two nuclear weapons for $20 million, which the general accepted without a second thought, given that all the weapons would soon be returned to Moscow.

The day after the nuclear weapons were removed from the base, Kasym lost his job, which was irrelevant because he was now on Al Hakim's payroll. Following Kasym's disassociation from the Russians, the imam told his followers that Kasym had killed General Vitaly Barinov and had been the imam's mole within the base, which was a considerable stretch of the truth but nevertheless accepted as fact by his followers since it came from the religious leader of their mosque. After that, Kasym became a respected elder within the community.

Two and a half decades later, at the age of sixty-five, Kasym was still caring for the weapons he'd stolen and fully expected to die before they left his charge. That assumption abruptly changed one cold winter day when someone he'd never seen before came to his door and gave him a rectangular cardboard box. When Kasym opened it, he saw a large sum of cash, a set of engineering drawings, and a note that he deciphered using an OTP that had been given to him some time ago. Kasym's knees weakened when he read that a man named Jabir Samara, along with four others, would take possession of the two nuclear weapons the following day. He was to use the enclosed cash to purchase two large cargo trucks and have them modified according to the enclosed drawings and to obtain the supplies listed below.

Kasym unconsciously turned and looked out the back window of his kitchen to a detached garage thirty yards in the distance, beneath which the two nuclear weapons were hidden. He had dug the chamber himself and used an overhead hoist to lower the weapons onto specially constructed platforms that could support the 2,220-pound weight of each weapon, each of which was thirteen inches wide and forty-eight inches long.

Nuclear devices required continual maintenance because plastic and rubber components, onboard batteries, and semiconductor electronic parts tended to degrade over time. Moreover, they were difficult to replace because, given the age of both weapons, manufacture of these parts had long ago ceased. That meant Kasym could obtain the parts only by cannibalizing existing weapons. Although the late General Barinov had given him a generous supply of replacement components, Kasym had used the last of them nearly a decade ago. Thankfully, through a friend at Pakistan's Atomic Energy Commission, and for a substantial sum of money, which Al Hakim had wired, he had been able to obtain what he needed.

Kasym brought his attention back from the garage. Rereading the note, he memorized the list of items he was to obtain and then took out a cigarette lighter and destroyed both the message and the OTP.

Prince Mahamat bin Salman was minister of the interior for Saudi Arabia. As such, he had control over his country's national security, naturalization, immigration, and customs. At six foot four he was tall for a Saudi and towered over other members of the royal family. In his early fifties, he was clean-shaven except for a thick black mustache, and the muscular two-hundred-pound royal had a physique similar to that of actor Tom Selleck.

Today he had been particularly busy. Now, at nine in the evening, he had just finished a meeting with the American Secretary of Homeland Security, and he was bone-tired. But sleep would have to wait because he needed to return to his office to review the correspondence and emails that had accumulated during his absence. The king had a habit of calling bin Salman when he least expected it, and he needed to be on top of what was happening within the kingdom in case he was asked.

The prince drove into the underground parking area of the Ministry of the Interior building and took his private elevator to the top floor. Once inside his office, he read through the raft of documents his assistant had placed on his desk, then turned on his computer and checked his emails. He saw that he'd received a message from Ahmed al-Khobar. Although there was no text, the email contained two attachments, one a video and the other a file of photos. He decided to look at the video first. The resolution was good, and he zoomed in on the two figures standing in front of an old run-down structure. One of the faces was Al Hakim's, which was to be expected since al-Khobar had been sent to follow him. The second belonged to someone the prince had hoped was dead. The prince's jaw tightened, and his eyes narrowed. He knew that the sight of a member of the Saudi royal family standing beside the world's most infamous terrorist would be disastrous for his country's relationship with the West. Taking his cell phone off his desk, he called Fareed Al Dossari, head of his General Investigation Directorate.

"Mesah al-khair, As-salaamu 'alaykum," the prince said, bidding Al Dossari a good evening and wishing peace upon him.

"As-salaamu 'alaykum," Al Dossari responded, sounding surprised to be receiving a call from his boss this late in the evening.

Al Dossari was a short man with a black goatee and mustache that were beginning to show his age with an intrusion of gray. He was five feet, six inches tall, with a leathery face that had been tanned and hardened by the desert winds. At 140 pounds, his body was well toned for a man in his early sixties, thanks mainly to a grueling two-hour daily workout that started at 5:00 a.m. The directorate had long been his home away from home. Al Dossari had worked his way through the hierarchy for thirty years before being promoted to his current position five years ago.

"We have a serious issue," the prince said following their initial greetings. He then went on to explain the video he had received from Ahmed al-Khobar. "I want to be notified when Al Hakim withdraws large sums of cash. If he wires funds from his bank accounts, find out where they're sent. To be clear, I don't want to stop the withdrawals, merely find out where this money is going."

"Understood. I'll set up around-the-clock electronic and visual surveillance of him and notify every financial institution in the kingdom of this requirement immediately," Al Dossari replied.

"We'll discuss this situation in more detail in my office at eight."

Al Dossari confirmed the time of the meeting, and the prince ended the call without further comment.

Normally, the prince would order Al Dossari to bring someone suspected of this type of crime to one of several locations the government used for questioning suspects. The reason for this was that surveillance was slow, tedious, and sometimes unreliable, such as when a suspect slipped away unnoticed. But the truth always came out in torture, and Saudi Arabia wasn't hamstrung by the same humanitarian rules of interrogation that bound many other nations. Al Hakim was an exception, however, because he was a member of the Saudi royal family. Even though he was at the lower end of that hierarchy, the prince couldn't subject him to torture unless he had absolute proof he'd acted against the nation.

Bin Salman took a pad of paper from the top drawer of his desk and began making bullet points regarding what he knew about Al Hakim's activities and the actions he'd initiated with Al Dossari. Satisfied as to the completeness of his notes, he phoned the head of the royal family, the only person who had final judgment on the fate of a royal.

Abdul-Malik Kasym had just finished cleaning up after dinner and was in the process of making himself tea when he heard a knock on his door. It was uncommon in Peshawar for anyone to arrive at another person's home unannounced at night, so he grabbed a handgun from a kitchen drawer and went to see who was there.

Opening the door slowly, with his gun pointed out the narrow opening, he saw a tall, bearded man of around forty standing in front of him. Behind the man were four others, of average height and weight, in their early twenties. Jabir Samara introduced himself, then gave the name of each of the men with him. Kasym relaxed upon hearing Samara's name, having been told to expect him in the note he'd received from

Al Hakim. He invited the five men inside. Before entering, each man took off his shoes and placed them beside the front door. They then followed Kasym to the dining room table, where he told them to relax while he went into the kitchen to make more mint tea. A short time later, he returned with the beverages.

"I'll begin obtaining the equipment and supplies you need tomorrow morning," Kasym said to Samara, without preamble. "It shouldn't take any longer than two to three days to modify the trucks and obtain the listed supplies."

"Will your neighbors be curious that you have visitors?"

"They won't say anything. Chechens are known for respecting the privacy of others and not inquiring into the matters of others. If our history has taught us anything, it's that getting involved in things that don't concern you can lead to an untimely demise."

Samara seemed satisfied with this response and took a sip of tea before setting the cup back down on the table. "Tomorrow at five, a messenger will arrive with a package," he said, looking at Kasym. "My men and I may be out at that time, looking at egress routes from the city. If we're not here, please receive it for me."

Kasym said that he would be home to receive the package if needed, his facial expression and demeanor indicating that he had no interest in knowing the contents of what was arriving. A short time later, everyone called it a night.

CHAPTER 3

I T BEGAN WITH an email from Fareed Al Dossari, sent an
hour following Al Dossari's call with the prince. Carrying
the seal of the Ministry of the Interior, the electronic
communication went to every financial institution in Saudi
Arabia and ordered the institutions to immediately phone
or text Chief Investigator Khalifa bin Nayef, at the number
provided, if Husam Al Hakim attempted to withdraw or wire
funds from any of his accounts. Al Dossari didn't have to
indicate that the email must be kept strictly confidential and
that Al Hakim should not be notified; the consequences for
an indiscretion involving something that the government
wanted to remain secret didn't have to be iterated.

The morning after the release of the message, a young,
well-dressed man in his midthirties named Nasser Boulos
entered the Banque Saudi Fransi carrying a large black travel
bag. He was five feet, nine inches in height, slender but not
thin, and clean-shaven, with black hair cut fashionably short.
Wearing a dark blue Brioni suit, open-collared white shirt,
and wing tip shoes, he looked like a banker or successful
businessman as he walked through the financial institution.

Boulos presented a check to the cashier, along with his
identification, and asked that the money be given to him in

American currency. The cashier looked at the amount of the draft and then directed Boulos to the office of the bank manager, indicating that the manager was the only one with the authority to approve cash withdrawals of this size.

The bank manager was sitting at his desk when the well-dressed man knocked on his open door and stated his business. The manager invited him to have a seat and then took the check from him. He requested and received two forms of identification and punched the account number printed on the check into his computer. Although the check had been issued by a company, Al Hakim's ownership of that company was reflected in the bank's computer system, which had been programmed early that morning per the instructions issued to the bank by the government. As a result, the instant the bank manager finished entering the account number, a bright red note appeared in the center of his computer screen, telling him to call Chief Investigator Khalifa bin Nayef at the provided cell phone number. This didn't come as a surprise because the manager had a printout of the email from Al Dossari on his desk.

"Because you have requested this in US currency," the manager said in an unhurried and reasonable voice, "it will take a few minutes to pull the funds from our vault. In the meantime, I'll take you to the executive lounge, where you can relax."

With no indication that he was suspicious about having to wait for the money, Boulos stood. It took a little longer for the manager to stand and join him, because he was copying the phone number on his computer screen into his cell phone before leaving his office.

After Boulos was comfortably seated in the lounge, the manager headed toward the vault, texting bin Nayef on his way. He provided the chief investigator with Nasser Boulos's name and the amount of the check from one of Al Hakim's accounts that he was trying to cash. Almost immediately, he received a reply telling him to ensure that Boulos didn't leave the bank for fifteen minutes.

Twelve minutes later, the manager received a second text, this one indicating that he should give the money to Boulos and let him leave.

Khalifa bin Nayef was on the short side at five feet, four inches tall. He was slender for a Saudi, tipping the scales at 120 pounds, twenty-five pounds or so less than average. He had opal-black eyes, a thin-lipped mouth, light brown skin, and a stare that seemed as if it would pierce steel. He was articulate and smart and was typically underestimated, because of his stature, by those he investigated. Sitting in his car across the street, he saw Boulos leave the bank carrying a large black travel bag in his right hand and hail a taxi. He recognized the man because he'd accessed the kingdom's citizen database and had Boulos's photo and personal information displayed on his cell phone. The chief investigator followed the taxi to the Riyadh King Khalid Airport and saw Boulos enter the international departures terminal. Pulling his car to the curb in a no-parking zone, he placed a Ministry of the Interior placard on the dash and followed the man inside.

Boulos was at the Aeroflot ticket counter when bin Nayef entered the terminal. The departure board to his right showed that the next Aeroflot flight was scheduled to depart for Grozny in forty minutes. The next flight after that didn't leave for four hours. Bin Nayef waited until Boulos left the counter and then also purchased a ticket to Grozny.

Since midday had the greatest number of departures, every queue for passport control and security was long. The placard near where Boulos was standing indicated that the wait time from that point was approximately thirty minutes. Seeing this, bin Nayef showed his credentials to one of the ticket agents and asked to see the head of airport security. The ticket agent, who had a direct line to security, complied. After a brief call, she directed bin Nayef to an office on the second floor.

Within the country's security apparatus, the Ministry of the Interior, and particularly the office of the chief investigator, were a big deal. When bin Nayef entered and presented his credentials, the head of security snapped to attention. With no time for pleasantries, the chief investigator told the five feet, seven inches tall, slightly rotund man in his forties that he needed to see what was inside the travel bag of someone who would be going through security but that it must be done without the person becoming suspicious. He also added that neither the man nor the bag was to be physically searched, and under no circumstances was he to be detained. The head of security acknowledged these instructions and typed a series of commands on his keyboard, which split his computer screen into six windows, each showing a scanning station within the terminal. Boulos was in the line closest to the Aeroflot ticket counter, and after bin Nayef pointed him out, the head of security left his office and rushed downstairs.

By the time Boulos got to the front of the queue, the head of security had been sitting in a chair looking at the x-ray images of passengers' luggage for ten minutes. Therefore, when Boulos placed his bag flat on the conveyor belt, everything seemed routine. Once the scan of the bag was complete, the security director left his chair and, apologizing to the well-dressed man, said that he had been distracted by one of his colleagues and hadn't looked at his computer screen. Without further explanation he picked up the bag and carried it back to the conveyor belt, but this time he placed it upright.

The well-dressed man, who was already through the metal detector and looking at his watch because his plane was getting perilously close to leaving without him, didn't question the rescan—probably because that would have called attention to both him and the bag. Once the bag completed its second pass, and no one prevented him from picking it up, Boulos let out a deep breath and, with his plane seven minutes from departure, began running to his gate.

The head of security immediately returned to his office and brought up both scans of the bag on his desktop. Bin Nayef didn't see anything unusual in the first image, but the second showed the faint outline of what appeared to be tight packets of money inside false compartments on both the sides and at the bottom of the bag.

"That bag weighed much more than it should," the head of security said. "If it hadn't been for your instructions, I would have taken it apart. I wonder how many times he's taken money out of the country in this manner."

"Thank you for your assistance," bin Nayef said, ignoring the question as well as any discussion on the contents of the bag. "This favor won't be forgotten."

With the flight to Grozny leaving in mere minutes, the head of security called ahead to ensure that the aircraft doors wouldn't be closed before bin Nayef's arrival. The chief investigator was transported to the gate by an electric cart, and after he presented his ticket to the agent and boarded, the door slammed shut behind him.

The plane landed in Grozny thirty minutes early thanks to the director of security at Riyadh, who had told the tower to give it departure preference, prioritizing the aircraft in front of the fourteen other planes waiting for takeoff. After disembarking, bin Nayef followed Boulos through customs and immigration and maintained visual contact as Boulos went to the auto rental center. The well-dressed man then left the airport, with the chief investigator following three cars behind.

Grozny was a small city, where one could drive from one end to the other in twenty-five minutes. It was also somewhat unique in that most of the homes had been built by their occupants or a former owner. The path that Boulos took skirted the center of the city, with its multitude of five- to nine-story apartment buildings and several high-rise structures. Fifteen minutes after leaving the airport, he entered an old neighborhood in what locals referred to as the private sector, an area of residences encircling the city's urban core, and parked in front of a small home with a detached garage in the back. Bin Nayef stopped his vehicle fifty yards from the home and watched. It was 5:00 p.m.

Boulos took his carry-on bag to the front door and knocked. After waiting a minute, he knocked again, this time with more vigor. Another minute passed, and still no one answered. He decided to look for the person to whom he was to deliver the money. Walking into the backyard, which was shielded from the neighbors by beech trees that lined three sides of the property, he went past an aging black Daihatsu Charade, a mini Japanese four-door with a one-liter engine, that was parked in the driveway. Twenty feet in front of it were two eight-foot-tall wooden doors that led into a large rectangular garage. Boulos pulled opened the door on the right and walked inside.

The interior was dark except for a large rectangular pit in the center of the structure, from which light was emanating. Curious, he softly walked to the edge and looked down. What he saw both surprised and horrified him—in the center of the pit were two large bombs resting on wooden platforms. Between them was a man in a radiation suit, which led Boulos to the inescapable conclusion that these were nuclear weapons.

Boulos hurried back to his vehicle and waited forty-five minutes before he again approached the home and knocked on the front door. When a man answered, Boulos handed over the travel bag without saying a word and returned to his car. Wishing to put as much distance between himself and the nuclear weapons as possible, he put the pedal to the metal on his return to the airport.

The chief investigator had watched Boulos knock on the front door and then walk around the side of the house to the backyard. From where he was parked, bin Nayef didn't have much of a view of the rear of the residence and could see only a sliver of the garage. Therefore, if he wanted to find out what Boulos was up to, he had to get much closer. Once the well-dressed man was out of sight, bin Nayef left his car and ran to the side of the house, just as Boulos was entering the garage. He continued his sprint to the far side of the garage where he was able to cover its entrance without being seen. He'd just gotten settled in that position when Boulos exited, closed the doors behind him, and ran in the direction of his vehicle. Whatever he had seen had apparently spooked him enough that he'd determined it was in his best interest to run rather than walk. After waiting several minutes to make sure that no one else was coming out of the building, bin Nayef entered the garage and closed the doors behind him. The inside was dark except for a light coming from a subterranean chamber in the center. Walking to the edge, bin Nayef looked down and saw what undoubtedly had caused Boulos to run. Taking his cell phone from his pocket, he took several photos.

Abdul-Malik Kasym was just about finished. The job had taken him longer than expected, and he was hurrying, realizing that by now the messenger either must be waiting or would be here at any moment. However, what he was doing couldn't be rushed because both weapons had to be perfect prior to their journey, and the problem he'd diagnosed with one of their sensors required a time-consuming recalibration. Kasym was glad that Samara and his men had decided to familiarize themselves with their route for leaving the city and hadn't yet returned because he didn't like anyone looking over his shoulder when he was working on the weapons, and he was sure they'd be doing just that from above if they were here.

The radiation suit he was wearing was hot and restrictive and would have been unnecessary if he were dealing with just the weapons-grade uranium core. In fact, one could hold the core with bare hands, and the body wouldn't absorb any of its radioactivity. That was because the alpha particles it emitted lost their energy very quickly and therefore had a short range. In fact, the particles weren't even able to penetrate the epidermis layer of skin. Moreover, the radioactive core was well shielded, and therefore there was little chance of radiation exposure. However, the radiation suit was necessary for the polonium-210 powder he'd spread around the interior of the weapons because that tasteless substance could be inhaled and ingested. It was 250,000 times more poisonous than hydrogen cyanide, which meant that if an amount as small as a grain of salt got into the body, the result would always be fatal.

Al Hakim had made it clear to Kasym that he didn't want any of the men who'd be transporting the weapons to survive because they could potentially implicate him. That created a timing problem, in that they needed to be alive when they planted the weapons but dead right after, even though none of the four would be around for the explosion. The polonium-210 powder that Kasym had earlier stolen from the base, in the expectation that someday he might be able to assassinate a top Russian official in revenge for the murder of his sons, was his solution to that problem.

To effectuate Al Hakim's plan, he would divide the four men accompanying Samara into two-man teams, with each team responsible for arming their bomb. Unknown to those transporting the weapons, arming the weapons would also simultaneously activate an internal timer that couldn't be stopped or reset. Therefore, detonation was assured. According to the plan that Kasym devised, arming would involve one man from each team removing the faceplate on their weapon, a task that was made easy by the butterfly fasteners over the access screws. Once inside the device, that person would flip a switch, which was coated with polonium-210 powder. To divert attention from the fine granules of radioactive material, Kasym would tell the men that they should expect to touch the antimoisture powder that he had used to protect the circuitry. The second person on the team would be poisoned after he reaffirmed that the weapon was armed, by ensuring the switch was in the up position.

Samara would be the hardest person to kill because he might consider it suspicious that the arming switches would need to be checked a third time and therefore might decide that twice was enough. Nevertheless, since all five men had to touch the radioactive substance within a narrow window of time to ensure they died within hours of each other, Kasym had to ensure Samara would do so. Thus, Kasym would tell Samara that there was a message for him next to the switch in each weapon, which his cousin Afridi had asked Kasym to place there. The messages, verses from the Koran, would hopefully allay his suspicions. The last step to ensure the weapons' detonation called for Samara to remove and discard the butterfly fasteners. Without them, no one would be able to access the internal workings of the bombs without drilling out each screw, a time-consuming process that could not be accomplished prior to the explosions.

When Samara and his men returned, having familiarized themselves with their primary and alternate routes out of the city, Kasym informed them of the delivery, pointing to the carry-on bag on the floor. Wordlessly, Samara lifted the bag onto the broad seat of the wooden chair nearest to him, slit the interior lining with his pocketknife, and pulled out the fat stacks of currency. After confirming that the amount matched his expectations, he returned the money to the bag and put it back on the floor.

"When do we get to see the bombs?" Samara asked, looking at Kasym, who was standing to his right.

"Now would be an opportune time since I just finished my final inspection." Kasym then led the five men out of the house and into the garage, where he used an overhead electric gantry crane to pick up the four heavy rectangular sheets of lead that covered the opening in the dirt floor. Once those were moved aside, he flipped a switch on the wall. Immediately, the chamber beneath the garage illuminated and exposed a ladder inside the chamber. Kasym was the first to descend, followed by Samara and then the other four men.

Once they were below, the four men accompanying Samara seemed mesmerized by the two nuclear weapons resting in V-shaped wooden cradles, although they all kept their distance and stood against the back wall of the chamber.

Kasym, sensing their reluctance to get closer, approached one of the weapons and placed his hands on it. "The radioactive core is well shielded, and therefore there's little chance of radiation exposure, even when you place a hand inside to arm the bomb. Touch it if you like."

Each of the five terrorists, who probably viewed cowardice as an affliction equal to the plague, came forward and put a hand near Kasym's. Once the lovefest with the nuclear weapon was over, they formed a semicircle around Kasym.

"How heavy are these?" Samara asked, looking at the four-foot-long, thirteen-inch-wide nuclear devices.

"Each bomb weighs slightly more than twenty-two hundred pounds," Kasym answered.

"And how do we get them on and off the trucks?"

"With a forklift. I'll purchase it in the next day or two, and you'll transport it in the back of one of the trucks. It'll comfortably lift over six thousand pounds, more than twice the weight of the bombs."

Kasym went on to explain that he'd covered the walls and ceiling of this chamber with sheets of lead not because the nuclear devices leaked a dangerous amount of radiation, but to ensure that airborne or satellite detectors wouldn't detect even a trace amount of radioactivity. He then explained for the next thirty minutes the mechanics of handling the weapons and the two-team approach he'd devised to activate the devices.

"Tomorrow I'll purchase the transport vehicles and bring them to a carpenter friend of mine, who'll construct a secret compartment in each, where you will hide the weapons."

"Won't your friend become suspicious and ask questions?" Samara asked.

"He'll think we're smuggling contraband across the border into Kazakhstan, a common enterprise among us Chechens. Once he's finished making the modifications to the vehicles, we'll remove the lead shielding from this chamber and line the compartments in the trucks. As you already know, your cover is that you're truck drivers transporting construction supplies. You'll also be carrying contraband—cartons of cigarettes and cases of alcohol, which will give the border officials something to find if they search the vehicles and which you can use for bribes as needed. Your construction supplies—bags of concrete, sand, and rocks—will be at the very back of the trucks."

"And the documentation for our journey?" Samara asked.

"The five of you have your passports?"

Samara nodded.

"Good. You'll have three sets of license plates and ownership papers for the vehicles before you leave."

"How long will all this take?"

"Not more than three days, which conforms with the timetable I've been given."

Several more questions followed, after which everyone left the chamber and returned to the house.

CHAPTER 4

WHEN BOULOS GOT to the airport, he returned his rental car, checked in for his flight, and immediately went to find a drink—something he wouldn't be able to do once he landed in Saudi Arabia. Although the bar was crowded, he found a stool and ordered a double Grey Goose vodka on the rocks to try to erase what he'd seen. By the fifth round, he was feeling no pain. In some other countries, he would have been considered too inebriated to board the aircraft. If that standard were enforced in Grozny, which was part of Russia, half the passengers boarding would have been turned away. And so, after being assisted to 23C by a male flight attendant, Boulos slumped back in his seat and passed out. Ten rows behind the inebriated messenger, bin Nayef watched.

When the plane landed in Riyadh, bin Nayef followed the disembarking passengers to passport control. Going to the VIP line, he showed his credentials to the immigration officer and told him to summon the head of security. Several minutes later, the same person who'd helped bin Nayef x-ray Boulos's bag arrived, and after finding out what bin Nayef wanted, he sent the immigration official away and took over his booth.

Ten minutes later, Boulos entered the immigration queue, assisted by the same flight attendant who'd taken him to his seat. After an identifying nod from bin Nayef, the head of security waved the two to the VIP line and swiped their passports through the reader attached to the government's computer system. He gave Boulos's passport special attention, hitting F6 on his keyboard as the document went through the reader and thereby requesting from the national database information on the person in question. Thirty seconds later, as the well-dressed man was on his way to customs, a great deal of information on Nasser Boulos started pouring from the laser printer in the immigration booth. Once complete, the twenty-page data dump was handed to the chief investigator.

It was nine thirty when bin Nayef left the airport and drove to his office. After writing a detailed report and attaching the photos he'd taken, along with a scanned copy of the data dump he'd received on Boulos, he emailed the file to Fareed Al Dossari. It was almost midnight when he shut down his computer and nearly 1:00 a.m. when he got to his residence. With his eyes at half-mast, his plan was to sleep until six, but that plan evaporated at 4:45 a.m. when Al Dossari phoned and told him to throw on some clothes and get to his office as quickly as possible. An hour later, he entered the General Investigation Directorate.

Prince Mahamat bin Salman had just finished rereading bin Nayef's report for the second time when Al Dossari and his chief investigator arrived at the prince's office and sat in the two chairs in front of his desk. The rapidness with which the meeting had been set was due solely to Al Dossari's enlarged prostrate. Not able to sleep longer than two hours at a time without going to the bathroom, he had the habit of keeping his computer on all night and reading all incoming emails after relieving himself. Therefore, after reading bin Nayef's report, he had immediately called the prince, who in turn had set the 6:00 a.m. meeting upon being given the *Reader's Digest* version of the report.

The prince, as was his habit, got straight to business without preamble. "I believe that my cousin's delivery of a great deal of money to someone in Grozny, coming on the heels of his meeting with Awalmir Afridi, means that they're planning one or more acts of terror. I also assume, since two nuclear weapons are hidden under this person's garage, that the attack will involve the detonation of these devices. Under no circumstances can we allow that to happen. My cousin's involvement with Afridi means, by extension, that the House of Saud is also responsible for whatever transpires between them."

"Would you like me to arrest your cousin?" Al Dossari asked.

"Not yet. The proof must be beyond refute, or nearly so, when someone in my family is involved. Perhaps the drunkard on the plane can tell us something," the prince said, referring to Boulos. "I also want an investigation into the disappearance of Ahmed al-Khobar, whom I haven't heard from since receiving his videos and photos from Peshawar."

"I'll start on both immediately," Al Dossari said. "I'll also have Khalifa arrange for someone to interrogate the person who received the money."

"Make sure he doesn't survive the interrogation. I need enough information from this person to confront my cousin, but I also want to get rid of anyone who can incriminate a member of the family."

"And what should we do with the nuclear weapons once he's killed?"

"Leave that to me."

It was just past two in the morning when Akhmad Umarov, a five foot seven, 270-pound Russian Chechen, stood in the backyard of the property behind Kasym's residence and looked at the row of beech trees with an eight-foot-high chain-link fence in front of them. Twenty years earlier, he would have scaled the fence in a snap. Now, having just turned forty-five, and with a complete lack of exercise over the past two and a half decades, his body's musculature was doing all it could to get him from his vehicle to a restaurant and move a fork to his mouth.

Dismissed as an interrogation specialist for Russian intelligence two months before his twenty-fifth birthday because the country's leadership at the time didn't trust Chechens, especially one inside the tent of one of its intelligence agencies, Umarov subsequently had become a private detective. Although his skills as an interrogator were known to his peers and those in competing intelligence functions, he was rarely hired to use that expertise. Instead, his bread-and-butter assignments involved taking photographs of unfaithful spouses. Then just last night he had received a call from someone who worked at the Saudi Arabian embassy in Moscow. The caller indicated that he knew of Umarov's interrogation skills and wanted a job done ASAP. He offered to triple the investigator's normal rate and pay in cash, and Umarov immediately agreed.

Earlier, after driving past Kasym's home, Umarov had made a tactical decision to enter through the rear rather than the front of the residence, since the front door faced a row of houses across the street and was well lit. Entering through the back meant less chance of being noticed. However, that decision produced its own set of problems: scaling the backyard fence was substantially harder than he'd anticipated, and after three attempts he still wasn't able to get over it.

Umarov hadn't always had the physique of a donut. His transition from average to obese had begun shortly after he lost his job as a Russian interrogator. That had started the ball rolling, and as his physical condition deteriorated over the years, his doctor had cautioned that he was cruising toward a heart attack if he didn't start exercising and dieting. He had ignored that advice because, as he put it, the cure was worse than the disease, so his body hadn't been asked to do anything this physically stressful for two decades. Bathed in sweat and breathing as if he'd just run a marathon, he took a few seconds to regain his breath. As he was doing so, he saw a pile of rocks near him and had a flash of ingenuity. Piling them atop one another, he gained nearly two feet in height and was able to grab hold of a beech tree branch that intruded into the neighbor's yard. Getting onto the limb, he pulled himself toward the fence, taking in deep gulps of air as he slowly made his way into Kasym's yard. His arms and legs were covered with sap, or whatever the tree limb produced to get even with him for being debarked.

Once over the fence, Umarov jumped to the ground, somehow managing to land and remain on his feet. That position was short-lived, however, because a second later a wave of nausea overcame him, and he grabbed his stomach, fell to his knees, and vomited. Beginning to sweat profusely, he couldn't seem to get enough air inside him and started gasping. Sitting down on the ground, he felt hot to the point of discomfort and removed his jacket and sweater to cool himself down. That's when his right arm began to hurt, and he suddenly felt an immense pressure on his chest. Seconds later, he fell on his back and stopped breathing.

It was early morning when Kasym, walking toward his garage with a backpack full of money, noticed a fat man lying on the ground near the back fence. The white pallor of the man's skin and his wide-open eyes and mouth indicated that Kasym was looking at a corpse. Returning to the house, he summoned Samara and his men to see if they recognized the man. All five shook their heads in the negative.

"As obese as he was, and with no obvious wounds, it was probably a heart attack," Samara said, searching the man for identification but finding none.

"He doesn't look like a thief," Kasym said.

"There's tree sap on his pant legs and arms, which probably means that he used that branch to get over the fence," Samara said, pointing to the limb extending into the neighbor's yard. "You can see the pile of rocks under it. There's no way he was going to scale the fence with that anchor of fat around his midsection. As unlikely as it seems, it appears he was a thief."

"I don't want to call the police because there's always a chance they could decide to look around. If that happens, there's no guarantee they won't find the chamber under the garage. There's also a possibility that someone will see us if we transport and dump the body elsewhere. It'll be safer if we bury him in the backyard."

Samara agreed and directed two of his men to begin digging a grave in a corner of the yard. By late morning, the man's body was six feet under the earth.

While Samara and his men were taking care of the body, Kasym got into his aging Daihatsu Charade and went to see a real estate agent he'd spoken to earlier, in order to negotiate the lease for a warehouse several miles from his residence. He gave no explanation as to its intended use, and none was expected. He then drove to the central marketplace, where anything, licit or illicit, could be bought for a price. The person he saw had a reputation for being able to obtain anything—for a price. After twenty minutes of haggling, he had negotiated the purchase of two modified M35 military vehicles.

The M35 was a two-and-a-half-ton cargo truck that weighed 13,000 pounds and was a little over nine feet high, eight feet wide, and twenty-three feet long. A fleet of them had been sent to Pakistan years ago as part of a military assistance package from the United States. To the naked eye, these M35s looked like any of the other ten-wheel former military vehicles that were now hauling civilian cargo. What made the two trucks he was purchasing unique, however, was that they had been modified to be multi-fuel, meaning they could use gas, diesel, and some types of aircraft fuel. Moreover, each had a fifty-gallon fuel tank, providing a range of up to five hundred miles. At the same time, Kasym purchased a hoist and a forklift capable of lifting three tons. The seller agreed to deliver everything to the warehouse at 5:00 p.m.

The carpenter was next on the list, and Kasym drove to his house, which was ten minutes from his own residence. After looking at the engineering drawings that were presented to him, which gave the specifics of how the secret compartment was to be constructed in the rear of the driver's cab of each truck, as well as the heavy-duty shock absorption system that was to be placed under each, the carpenter gave Kasym a price. Five minutes of haggling followed, after which a stack of US dollars, the currency of choice for illicit transactions, was handed over. With one last stop to make, Kasym drove to a warehouse not far from his and purchased building materials, alcohol, and tobacco to fill the storage area of each truck. With the backpack of money nearly depleted, he returned home.

Being summoned by the General Investigation Directorate was said to make even the bravest person break out in a sweat and sometimes wet his pants. The king allowed the agents of the directorate, referred to domestically as the Mabahith, to operate with impunity. Arbitrary arrests, incommunicado detention, and torture that included waterboarding and worse were commonplace in the Mabahith's interrogation rooms within Riyadh's Ulaysha Prison.

Nasser Boulos was handcuffed to a chair when Fareed Al Dossari entered. The surrounding room was twelve by twelve feet and had seafoam-green walls that had lost their luster decades ago. In the center was a rusting black metal table, on either side of which were similarly aging metal chairs. All were firmly bolted to the floor. In contrast to his usual dapper appearance, the previously well-dressed man was unshaven and wearing a drab gray prison jumpsuit and slippers.

"Do you know why you're here?" Al Dossari asked as he sat down opposite Boulos.

"I don't," he responded in the humblest of tones. "I've broken no laws."

"That's your first lie. This time I'll let it pass. But in the future, there will be severe consequences for not telling the truth. The answer to my question is that you illegally transported money out of the country. This is a crime for which I could have you beheaded."

Boulos began to sweat and squirmed in his seat. "I believed that I'd been given royal approval. Otherwise, I'd never have done this."

"You mean Husam Al Hakim's approval?" Al Dossari asked.

"Yes."

"Still, our laws are very clear. Only the king can grant such approval. Given that you've already admitted your guilt, there's no need to take up our court's time with a defense that's nonexistent. Since the executioner works in this building, I plan to be merciful and not prolong your anguish. I'll have you kneeling in front of him within five minutes." Al Dossari turned to the guard at the back of the room and said, "Begin preparations."

The guard immediately left and closed the door behind him.

Boulos looked like he was about to faint. "Be merciful," he pleaded in a sobbing voice.

"Mercy? How do I extend mercy to a criminal who's made no amends and tells me nothing?"

"I will tell you everything. Everything!"

The guard returned and whispered in Al Dossari's ear, after which Al Dossari told him to wait outside.

"You'll have one chance to tell the truth," Al Dossari said. "Leave nothing out because your life, literally, depends on it."

Boulos spent the next hour telling him everything.

CHAPTER 5

HUSAM AL HAKIM had met his distant cousin Prince bin Salman only once. He had always wanted to socialize with the hierarchy of the royal family, but he was too far down the family tree of the House of Saud to warrant that. Therefore, not having spoken to bin Salman for some time, he was surprised when Fareed Al Dossari came to his office, just before he was to go to lunch, and asked that he accompany him to the Ministry of the Interior for a meeting with the prince. What was troubling about this invitation was that it was extended by the head of the secret police—although the General Investigation Directorate didn't condone that name and discouraged its use in public. The fact that his cousin had sent Al Dossari to get him indicated that this meeting wasn't social, which seemed to be reconfirmed when Al Hakim saw three stout and unsmiling men standing next to a white S650 Mercedes with an open right passenger door. He climbed into the back seat and was soon wedged between two broad-shouldered escorts.

The drive to the ministry's headquarters on King Fahad Road took thirty minutes. The Mercedes pulled into the underground parking of the building that resembled a six-story brown flying saucer and stopped next to an elevator.

Al Dossari stepped out of the front passenger seat of the car and pointed his RFID card at an unseen sensor, after which both elevator doors opened. Upon seeing this, Al Hakim's escorts allowed him to exit the vehicle and enter the elevator ahead of them.

Getting off on the top floor, they passed through an atrium devoid of furniture or decoration, other than a highly polished white marble floor with the seal of the ministry in the center. Ten paces beyond, Al Dossari knocked on a highly polished set of mahogany doors. A voice called for them to enter, and the two escorts waited outside as Al Dossari and Al Hakim entered. Sitting in a black leather chair at the back of the room, behind a large glass desk, was Prince Mahamat bin Salman. The office was five hundred square feet, which was small by Saudi standards for an official of his standing. With the interior decorated in a minimalist style, the only other pieces of furniture within were the two chairs in front of the prince's desk.

The prince motioned for them to take a seat with a wave of his hand. The fact that his cousin didn't give him a traditional double kiss on the cheeks, as was customary between family members, seemed to set the mood for the meeting. Al Hakim's face became increasingly haggard, and his right arm developed a slight tremor as he waited in silence.

Thirty seconds later, the prince stopped working on his laptop and wordlessly handed his cousin an eight-by-ten photograph of him standing beside Awalmir Afridi outside the dwelling in Peshawar. The look on Al Hakim's face was a combination of surprise and fear. With a shaky hand, he leaned forward and laid the photo back on his cousin's desk.

"Would you like to explain this to me, cousin?" bin Salman asked in an even and tempered tone, which somehow managed to sound more threatening than if he had raised his voice.

"I support anyone who will kill the enemies of Islam."

"You're aware that his person was responsible for the kidnapping of the presidents of the United States and China? And you further realize that the kingdom depends on the United States for its general security? Funding someone who wants to assassinate world leaders is not in our national interest and therefore is considered treasonous."

"That's hypocrisy, cousin." Al Hakim spoke in a defiant tone, deciding that the best defense was a good offense. "There are many charities in this country that funnel money directly to our brothers who fight Israel and the United States, as well as give money to those who resist them. Will you deny that?"

The prince remained silent. No one had to remind him that the kingdom was the largest source of funds for Islamic militant groups, whose followers routinely entered the country disguised as holy pilgrims to solicit funds and receive assistance from government-sanctioned charities. They also set up front companies to launder money.

"Funding militant groups is one thing and altogether different from the assassination of foreign leaders. Setting that aside, however, you're here to explain why you funded the purchase of two nuclear weapons." Bin Salman placed in front of Al Hakim the photo that bin Nayef had taken of the devices.

Al Hakim stared at the grainy photo for a long time; it was the first time that he'd seen the bombs. "I didn't purchase these, cousin. You must be mistaken."

"Please, do you think I'm an idiot? You employed Nasser Boulos to withdraw US currency from one of your corporate accounts at the Banque Saudi Fransi and had him courier it to a residence in Grozny where these two weapons are being stored."

Al Hakim was uncharacteristically speechless, and the room was silent until the prince spoke again.

"Since you seem to be at a loss for words, perhaps the General Investigation Directorate can jog your memory." With a wave of his hand, the prince signaled that the meeting was over, and Al Dossari escorted his prisoner out of the room.

Prince Mahamat bin Salman's Mercedes Maybach S650 pulled onto the black marble tile in the parking area at King Turki bin Abdulaziz Al Saud's palace. Standing at a respectful distance to the side of the vehicle was the monarch's personal assistant, who would guide bin Salman through the labyrinth-like complex to the king's study. The prince did not really need an escort, since he'd been to the palace dozens of times, but the fact that the king sent his personal assistant and not a lower-level functionary was a sign of utmost respect.

The sand-colored palace, with a magnificent royal mosque beside it, was nestled between three lakes. These flanked extensive gardens and an enormous lagoon-shaped pool. The 317-room residence was adorned with 1,500 tons of Italian marble, silk oriental carpets, gold-plated faucets, and furnishings that could stand toe-to-toe with the interior of the Palace of Versailles. Yet the king eschewed most of these trappings from time to time for a 1,000-square-foot private study that, he said, was a welcome contrast to the opulence of the residence that had been built by his ancestors.

When the prince entered the dimly lit study, he saw the leader of the House of Saud sitting on a two-cushion lemon chiffon–colored couch and was directed to sit on the matching one across from him. The king was not known for exchanging small talk, so the prince got straight to the point. He took two photos from the envelope he was carrying and handed them to his sovereign. He then explained how a member of the royal family, Husam Al Hakim, was funding Awalmir Afridi and, more troubling, had purchased the nuclear weapons in the photos.

The king looked at the first photo, which showed someone dressed in radioactive protective gear, standing beside two bombs in an underground chamber. The serial number of each bomb was boldly stenciled in black across it. As the king studied the photo, the prince said that it was because of how the man was dressed that he believed these were nuclear weapons. The second photo was of Al Hakim and Afridi. The king's pallor whitened, and his goateed jaw became rigid as he stared at the photos.

"Earlier today, my cousin admitted to paying a Chechen to steal the nuclear weapons during the demise of the Soviet Union," said the prince. "Since then, he's been paying this person to maintain the nuclear devices. He's also reaffirmed that he's been a major funding source for Awalmir Afridi."

"If it's discovered that a member of the royal family purchased nuclear weapons and funded Awalmir Afridi's kidnapping of the presidents of the United States and China, such a revelation would be catastrophic for the kingdom. And if these devices are detonated, there won't be any discussion—only retaliation. It will destroy the House of Saud. How many people know about this?"

"The courier who transported the money to Grozny has committed suicide in his cell. My cousin, I'm sorry to say, had an undiagnosed heart condition, and the strain of questioning took its toll. That leaves only Awalmir Afridi, the person maintaining the weapons in Grozny, two of my staff, and myself."

"Our first task is to get hold of the weapons. Unfortunately, since they're on Russian soil, only the Russians can go after them. It would be an act of war for anyone else to seize the weapons. However, before we give them the location of the caretaker's home, we must eliminate him since he conspired with a member of the royal family. Otherwise, he'll tell the Russians that your cousin with the weak heart coordinated the theft of these weapons, paid for their maintenance, and schemed with Awalmir Afridi to detonate them on Chinese soil."

"I've already given that order. However, I haven't heard from the contractor that the kill was successful, and all efforts to contact him have failed."

"Don't leave such an important task to a foreigner. Send your most trusted person, and not a contract killer, to eliminate this caretaker. I want to keep this matter within a tight circle. That still leaves Awalmir Afridi. Any suggestions on how we kill him?"

"Several, but we have to locate him first."

Samara and his men left Grozny on schedule and three hundred miles later crossed into Azerbaijan, a country that bordered the Caspian Sea, which was the dividing line between Europe and Asia and the largest inland body of water on Earth. Just before reaching the border, Samara had put Azerbaijan license plates on each vehicle and thrown away the old license plates and vehicle registrations. Afridi believed that changing the plates and registrations prior to each border crossing would lessen the chance that they could be tracked, and the trucks would attract less attention since the plates were domestic. Samara's ability to speak the language of each of the countries they'd be in, except for China, was yet another layer of security meant to deflect attention from their journey.

Russia was now behind them, and their next stop, the Azerbaijan city of Baku, was just ahead. All five men were hungry, exhausted, and in need of sleep. What should have been an easy seven-hour drive from the border to Baku had taken twice that long, due solely to Azerbaijan border control. Apparently, the civil servants on duty were in no hurry to expedite the travel of others. It had taken two hours for Samara to receive and fill out the required documents, after which he had waited an additional two hours in an uncompromising wooden chair for the only person who could approve them to come back from whatever it was that he was doing. After Samara paid a bribe, cloaked as a priority processing fee, a stamp was affixed to the signature page of each document, and Samara left the building.

Once he returned to the vehicles, both M35s had proceeded to the final checkpoint. There they had waited another two hours for a customs inspection. When the two inspectors finally showed up, both reeking of alcohol, one grabbed the paperwork from Samara's hands while the other proceeded into the rear of each vehicle and wordlessly removed a case of Russian vodka. Once this was done, the other inspector, who'd been holding the trucks' documentation, put his stamp in the required spot and cleared them to enter the country.

The drive to Baku was uneventful. However, the weather was significantly colder than they had expected, with the wind chill index nearing zero. The one thing that they had failed to do was check the weather along their route before they left Grozny, and that oversight now cost them in that they hadn't brought the proper clothing. The five men were miserable as they tried to get some semblance of warmth from the trucks' heaters, which had begun deteriorating twenty years earlier.

Following the route given on Samara's cell phone, they had no problem finding the Baku marine terminal, where they planned to take a ferry to Aqtau, Kazakhstan, a distance of 270 miles. Getting there early was important because Samara's research showed that the eighteen-hour voyage didn't have an exact time of departure. Instead, it left the dock when the ferry reached its capacity of passengers, vehicles, or cargo. Their previous timetable had called for them to arrive at the terminal two hours before departure. However, that ferry had long departed. The ferry that was currently at the dock was scheduled to leave in thirty-five minutes, at least according to its transit schedule in Google.

After Samara paid the transport costs and the five men presented their passports for review, both trucks were allowed on board and were the cork in the bottle, so to speak, taking up the last of the space for vehicles. The lower deck, where anything with a wheel was parked, was a wind tunnel of sorts, which meant that it was bone-chillingly cold. Samara had originally planned for everyone to sleep in the back of the trucks, but he hadn't counted on the temperature hovering near zero. As a result, he went up to the bursar's office and rented the last two staterooms, at triple their usual price. Samara took one room for himself and put his four men in the other. He then put together a schedule so that there would always be one person inside the back of each vehicle, rotating every three hours so that everyone would have a chance to get warm and take a short nap.

The crossing to Aqtau, Kazakhstan, went smoothly, and the ferry docked at 6:00 p.m. the following evening. Even though the weather at the port was nineteen degrees, it seemed warm in comparison to what they'd experienced on the ferry. More importantly, educated by their previous border crossing, they expedited their clearance through customs by giving both cigarettes and alcohol to the local officials and thereby left the port within an hour of their arrival.

The M35s were gas guzzlers, with the trucks' fuel gauges indicating that there was slightly less than a quarter of a tank remaining in each. Samara decided to wait until they got out outside Aqtau to find a gas station, so that he could switch the license plates from Azerbaijan to Kazakhstan away from prying eyes.

They left the city just as the sun was beginning to set and forty-five minutes later came upon a local market and fueling station in a small no-name town. Samara directed his driver to pull in behind a truck that was parked beside a row of fifty-five-gallon drums, where a man was using a hand-operated rotary pump to move fuel into his vehicle. A large wooden sign with the word "market" painted in large black letters hung over the door of what was obviously a residence. Both trucks pulled behind the one being refueled, and the five men entered the home, finding that the front of the residence had been converted into a retail space lined with shelves of packaged and unpackaged food items.

The unmistakable smell of *beshbarmak*, the national dish of Kazakhstan, permeated the air. Samara had ordered it several times at a Russian restaurant not far from his farm and found the boiled meat and noodles in onion sauce to be delicious. Looking into the adjoining kitchen, he saw a husband and wife preparing a large pot of it inside.

When the husband saw the five men, he came into the store and asked how he could be of service. Samara replied, in a rough voice that reflected his fatigue from the journey and cold weather, that he needed about seventy-five gallons of gas and five orders of beshbarmak, with two of the dishes held back until the men he was sending to refuel their vehicles returned. After requesting and receiving an advance payment for the fuel and the meals, the husband went into the kitchen to get their food.

Once the proprietor was gone, Samara directed two of his men to go back outside and change the license plates and then refuel the trucks once the driver ahead of them had finished. They'd be relieved as soon as their counterparts finished eating. The men returned to the trucks to do as they had been told. After changing the plates, they both climbed into the cab of their lead vehicle and turned on the engine to get whatever heat they could while waiting to refuel.

CHAPTER 6

TWO BOYS, AGED ten and twelve, quietly entered the rear M35 parked in front of the market and began rummaging around inside. Both had stolen goods from trucks parked outside their parents' home when drivers were too busy eating or refueling to notice them. Their father had taught them the fine art of thievery and emphasized that the secret to not getting caught was to get in and out quickly. Therefore, they were instructed to take "just a pinch," as he would say, which would almost always go unnoticed until the drivers were too far away from the market to determine that's where their goods had been pilfered. The brothers had taken their father's advice and, having stolen goods in this manner for over two years, had never come close to being caught.

Both boys were thin and flexible, which made getting around in the tight confines of a truck relatively easy. The older boy, who was slightly taller and had longer arms than his brother, immediately went after the cigarettes, which were worth more on the black market than the alcohol. Putting his pocket-size LED flashlight in his mouth, he shimmied up the stack of boxes, removing the top one and steadying it on his head with one hand as he maneuvered down to the bed of the truck. When he got there, he repeated the process, after which he moved both boxes to the rear of the vehicle. Not seeing his younger brother, he began looking for him, since their success was dependent on getting in and out of the truck quickly and without being noticed. Lingering meant getting caught. In this area of the world, that resulted in one's death as a warning to others, no matter a person's age.

He found his brother deeper into the truck, taking out screws from the wooden barrier behind the driver's cab. Holding his Swiss Army knife in one hand and his LED flashlight in the other, the younger boy had already removed six of the fifteen screws holding the barrier in place.

"This wood is new while the rest of the truck is old and worn," the boy said upon seeing his brother approach. "They're hiding something valuable behind here."

When the older brother looked closely, he saw that someone had tried to distress the wood to make it appear older. His brother was always good at noticing even the smallest detail or imperfection. "Or this replaced one that was damaged," his brother added as an alternative explanation. "I have what we came for. Let's go before we're seen."

"There's treasure behind here. I know it," the brother said, beginning to remove the next screw.

The older sibling shook his head. Bowing to his brother's stubbornness, he took out his own Swiss Army knife and began removing screws. When the last one was out, they pushed the sheet of wood back as far as they could, which was about a foot, and the older boy shone his light inside the hidden compartment. With the younger boy looking over his brother's shoulder, their eyes went wide at the sight of a large bomb resting on a wooden platform.

"It must be fake to keep anyone from looking inside," the younger brother said.

"We'll find out," said the older boy, who wasted no time in twisting the butterfly fasteners and removing the faceplate. Poking his light into the opening, he saw a two-position switch surrounded by heaps of powder and, next to it, wires running to various electronic components. Curious, he put his hand inside, hoping to find a hidden space. Finding none, he pulled his hand out and saw that it was covered in the coarse powder that surrounded the switch. Wondering if this was a drug that was being smuggled into the country, he licked it. It tasted bitter, and he quickly swallowed it. Equally curious, his younger brother put his hand into the opening, touched the powder, and similarly swallowed the bitter substance. Both concluded that since neither felt any different, what they had touched wasn't a drug.

Deciding it was time to leave, they quickly replaced the butterfly screws and put the partition back in place before making their way to the rear of the truck. Poking their heads out from under the tarp, they saw that the driver in the lead vehicle had finished at the pump and was getting into the cab of his truck. Throwing the contraband that they'd stolen on the ground, they jumped from the rear of the vehicle, picked up the boxes, and headed to the back door of the kitchen.

As they ran, their legs began to spasm, and just as they rounded the corner of the residence and were in sight of the back door, they collapsed to the ground and started throwing up. They were in too much agony to scream or call for help, and their stomach contractions were so severe that it was difficult for them to breathe. They stayed alive for ten minutes. The older brother was the first to die, eventually succumbing by choking on his vomit and suffocating to death, although a coroner could have listed a half dozen other medical issues that were simultaneously competing to be the cause of death. His younger brother died around the same time from internal bleeding, although, like his sibling, there were numerous medical issues simultaneously sucking the life from him.

As the boys were dying, the two drivers moved their trucks adjacent to the hand-operated rotary pump and began refueling. Unlike the driver ahead of them, who had refueled not only his truck but also myriad containers in his vehicle, they were able to move quickly, transferring approximately thirty-seven gallons of fuel into each M35.

Nuray Aliyev opened the back door a sliver and called for her sons to come in from the cold and eat. The boys were always hungry and seldom waited for a second invitation to enjoy their mother's cooking, unless they were carrying on the family's side business of pilfering the trucks parked outside while their drivers came in to grab food or filled their tanks with gas. When they failed to show up after several minutes, she still thought little of it and issued a second invitation, figuring they'd been busy and hadn't heard her the first time. It wasn't until they failed to come after her third call that she decided to go outside and get them.

Opening the back door, she saw both boys lying motionless on the ground ten feet in front of her, each with red vomit on and around them. Running to them, she gave each CPR, but neither responded. After screaming for her husband, who was doing prep work in the kitchen, she continued to try to resuscitate her sons. Once he joined her, and after a brief exchange of hysterics, they carried their sons to their SUV, which was parked twenty feet away on the side of the house. While the wife knelt beside them, alternating putting her mouth over the mouth of each of her sons and pounding their chests to try to get their hearts going, the husband raced to Regional Hospital #33 in Aqtau—the closest medical facility to them. With the boys' father driving at speeds of over one hundred miles per hour, what should have been a forty-five-minute journey took only thirty.

The SUV screeched to a halt in front of the emergency room entrance, and each parent rushed inside carrying one of the lifeless boys. The first nurse they encountered escorted them to a treatment room. Dr. Aleksandr Uglov, a Russian physician who'd married a Kazakh and moved to Aqtau, entered the room seconds later and examined the boys, after which he gently declared them dead to their parents.

"How long were your sons sick?" Uglov asked the father, who was trying to remain stoic, though tears rolled down both cheeks, as the mother wailed beside the bodies.

"They weren't sick. Two hours ago, they were playing, and now they're dead."

"Whatever killed them acted with lightning speed. Perhaps the boys ingested a poison, such as cyanide? It's inside the bait used to kill rats and other rodents."

"I store poison in my basement, and the boys know to stay clear of it," the father responded, trying to hold it together while his wife continued to weep between the two gurneys holding her sons.

Uglov nodded, accepting what the father said without question. "Again, what's unusual in this case is the speed of their deaths. I haven't seen a nonpoison kill this quickly since I was at Chernobyl. I'll know more once I perform the autopsy. Again, my deepest condolences."

"When can we take our sons home for burial?" the father asked, not knowing how long autopsies took.

"It could be as long as one to two weeks if a toxicology screen is needed. If not, several days. Not knowing what I'm dealing with, I'll move them to the quarantine wing and perform the autopsies there as a precaution. Until I determine the cause of their deaths, you and your wife will also have to be quarantined."

The husband, wife, and boys were placed in separate rooms in the isolation wing of the hospital. Uglov decided to start the autopsies immediately, beginning with the eldest boy, and he donned a hazmat suit. He began by making a Y-shaped incision and gradually worked his way down to the chest organs and digestive tract, where he took tissue, blood, and fluid samples, including urine from the bladder. He repeated this process on the younger son. Once the autopsies were complete, he hand-delivered the samples to both the histology and toxicology labs and asked them to expedite their analysis. Six hours later, he received both lab results.

Jabir Samara had relieved the two men pumping fuel once he had finished eating. Now he walked back into the market to pay the small amount of money that he owed for the two gallons of fuel he had pumped over his earlier estimate and found that the owners weren't there to accept his payment, nor were they in the adjoining kitchen. Instead, he found the two men who hadn't eaten earlier finishing their beshbarmak at the kitchen table.

"Where did the husband and wife go?"

"We don't know. We found some dishes and served ourselves," one of the men said, pushing his empty plate away from him.

"I'm not waiting for them to return. Let's go."

With that, the three men left the kitchen and walked to the front door, with Samara grabbing several boxes of packaged snacks off the shelves as he left. Seconds later, both trucks continued toward China.

The boys' histology and toxicology results indicated that no poisonous compounds had been found in either tissue or fluid samples. However, there was an extremely high level of thallium. Uglov thought back almost thirty years to the postmortem results of those who had died at Chernobyl, as well as the bloodwork of workers who had died in several unpublicized lab accidents that the government had kept under wraps. Since there was no nuclear reactor in the area—the closest was several hundred miles away—the boys must have somehow ingested or inhaled a radioactive substance that Moscow had officially never acknowledged yet nevertheless produced. There was no other way to account for both the exceedingly high levels of thallium in the deceased and their rapid demise. Fortunately, there was one way to be sure.

Going to his lab, Uglov retrieved the tubes of urine and blood that he'd taken from the older boy and drove to Caspian State University of Technology and Engineering. Some of the staff there were his patients, and they granted him access to the advanced equipment in the physics lab, allowing him to conduct tests that were beyond the capabilities of the hospital. Today he needed to use the alpha spectroscope. Although alpha radiation couldn't penetrate a sheet of paper, when ingested or inhaled it was like a bull in a china factory and destroyed living cells with reckless abandon. Given the high level of thallium in both boys, he believed that's what had killed them. The test he was about to conduct would either confirm or eliminate alpha radiation as the cause of death.

The tests took slightly more than an hour to run and positively concluded that both boys had died from ingesting polonium-210, exposure to which the parents would soon succumb if he didn't get them on a chelate protocol.

When Uglov returned to the hospital, the nurse in charge of quarantine told him that the mother was deteriorating rapidly. He put on a gown, gloves, and mask and entered her room. After a brief examination and review of her lab results, he ordered a blood and platelet transfusion. What he really needed, however, were two chelating agents—dimercaprol and penicillamine. And as far as he knew, only one place had both, and that place was in Moscow.

CHAPTER 7

T HE SATELLITE ORBITING far above Russia wasn't technically the property of the National Security Agency. Instead, it belonged to the National Reconnaissance Office, which designed, built, and operated all spy satellites for the United States government. This spy in the sky didn't take photographs. It conducted signals intelligence, or SIGINT in government jargon, eavesdropping on both Russian communications and electronic signals. It then forwarded what it recorded to a sprawling complex at Fort Gordon known as NSA/CSS Georgia. From there the data was routed to a massive exaflop-speed computer—a series of supercomputers with a staggering processing speed of a quintillion, or billion billion, operations per second. This system translated the incoming data, looking for specific keywords, phrases, or combinations of words requested by someone or considered hot buttons in the intelligence community. If exaflop found something, the information was forwarded to the relevant NSA analyst for review. If not, the data went into the agency's massive database where it could be extracted if its contents later were the subject of someone's search.

During the Cold War, the NSA's Russian analytical section had been the largest intelligence-gathering unit at the agency. Now, with the Middle East in turmoil, Afghanistan, Iraq, Libya, Iran, and their neighbors were the agency's priority. Libby Parra had been an analyst in the Russian section since January 1992. She had graduated with a degree in Russian studies and spoke and read the language like a native. More importantly, she thought like a Russian. Her reports, at one time, had routinely ended up on the president's desk, and the National Security Council routinely read Parra's reports prior to making strategic recommendations on anything related to Russia.

Never married, the statuesque blonde had retained her beauty as she aged. Many had compared her to Raquel Welch or Ursula Andress, and she had turned down more than a few marriage proposals over the years. What she wanted instead was a relationship without vows, feeling that it drew a couple closer when either person could leave when they felt the love between them was now an ember. Several men over the years had professed that this was exactly what they wanted, but all had changed their tune and proposed marriage at some point. After that, the relationships had ended. Her current partner had taken heed, and their relationship had so far lasted five years.

Parra had already put in her twenty and could retire whenever she decided to pull the plug. But she had no intention of leaving the NSA until someone sent in a stretcher to remove her corpse. This was her life and what made getting out of bed each morning worthwhile. Today her computer screen showed a dozen intercepts that the exaflop had forwarded to her for review. She worked her way through the first five before lunch and brought up the sixth after she returned to her desk with her sixth cup of coffee of the day. The last intercept was a cellular conversation between a doctor at Regional Hospital #33 in Aqtau, Kazakhstan, and his former supervisor in Moscow. After viewing the computer's English translation, Libby set aside her coffee and, typing in a series of commands, requested that the exaflop send her the actual conversation—since the translation didn't give her the stress, concerns, and other vocal interactions between parties.

"Are you sure it's polonium-210?" the medical group director asked, in a voice that questioned the caller's judgment.

"I'm certain only because of my previous experience with it." Uglov went on to explain the tests he'd conducted and the reasoning behind the conclusions that he'd drawn.

"You're seeing ghosts from the past, Aleksandr. If the Russian government did have polonium-210, I promise they wouldn't be storing it anywhere near Aqtau. You've made a mistake. The boys somehow ingested poison. The symptoms, as you know, can be deceptively similar."

"At one time I worked at the Borisoglebsk weapons storage facility outside Peski. While I was there, a technician dropped a container of polonium-210 and apparently inhaled some particles. His spectroscopic test results were the same as these two boys'. I realize this radioactive bastard of a creation doesn't officially exist, but you and I both know differently."

The connection between the two men was silent for a moment. "You said that the mother is deteriorating rapidly?"

"That's correct. She most likely tried to resuscitate her sons and ingested the radioactive material through mouth-to-mouth contact. She'll die unless the chelates are administered to her."

"And the boys died two days ago?"

"Three."

"And the father is fine?"

"At this point, he seems to be."

"Expect the chelates to arrive tomorrow by courier. As far as anyone is concerned, this person is a visiting doctor. I don't want anyone to know that Moscow is involved or even concerned by what happened to these people. It's a simple case of accidental poisoning. The last thing I need is curiosity and scrutiny. I don't have to tell you of the diplomatic ramifications and questions Moscow will receive and be unable to answer if word gets out that the boys died because of inhalation or ingestion of polonium-210. Let's treat your patients, get them well, and usher them out of the hospital with an explanation from you that their sons died of poisoning. Tell them you feel sorry for what happened and give them the cash we'll send. They'll believe it came from you, and the issue will stay local, with no mention of Moscow."

The call wrapped up less than a minute later.

The seventh message of the dozen that the exaflop had forwarded for Libby Parra's review was the supervisor using his cell phone to call a friend who worked in the administrative section of the FSB, the principal security agency in Russia and the successor to the KGB. At the very beginning of their conversation, however, there were two misunderstandings—one by each of them. The supervisor assumed that his friend's cell phone was encrypted. Not understanding cellular technology in the slightest, he didn't know that both devices needed to have compatible encryption capabilities for that to occur. The second misunderstanding, this one by the FSB officer, who had only a slightly better handle on technology than his friend, was that he was being called from an analog desk phone, which was the standard communications device in Russian government offices. Since desk phones were connected to hard landlines, it was difficult for anyone to tap into those conversations. The fact that the caller was not using his desk phone but a cellular device, and that it therefore had an airborne connection to a cellular tower atop the building, escaped the FSB officer. Therefore, both Einstein's spoke with reckless abandon as the FSB officer worked his way up his chain of command, asking his friend to explain to each person his earlier conversation with Uglov, until they eventually spoke with Vladimir Putin.

Colonel Vasily Kvachkov walked with an even cadence down the corridors of Regional Hospital #33. He wore a black business suit, white shirt, and red tie, the suit and shirt having been tailor-made in Russia. His black highly polished double monk strap wing tip shoes, however, had been handmade in Rome—purchased there when he was surveilling someone suspected of being a double agent. Since that assignment had ended in a highly successful outcome and had resulted in a promotion, these had become his de facto good-luck footwear and had been resoled twice over the years. Kvachkov was of average height and weight, with gray hair that was barely more than stubble. He wasn't a conversationalist, believing he could learn more about people by listening to them rather than engaging in banter or chitchat. That insight, he would tell subordinates in the FSB, illuminated both the strengths and weaknesses of a person. However, when he did speak, his baritone voice exuded competency and authority. He did have a uniform, as did the four FSB agents who had accompanied him on the flight and were now sitting in their rented SUV. However, since Kazakhstan was now a sovereign nation, and they had no legal or military jurisdiction here, everyone wore civilian clothes.

Kvachkov found Uglov's office and greeted him with a businesslike coldness that was part of his persona. His military training and FSB experience had long ago excised caring, empathy, and other traits perceived to be human frailties. Uglov seemed to know what to expect and, without shaking hands or pursuing further conversation, led the colonel to the hospital's quarantine ward, which was located on the bottom floor of the six-story hospital. That area had its own intake and exhaust airflows, air filtration systems, and pressure-differentiated rooms and a host of other features that made the escape of infectious particles extremely unlikely.

Upon their arrival, Uglov and Kvachkov changed into blue scrubs and donned head and shoe covers, surgical masks, and latex gloves. They entered the mother's room, finding Nuray Aliyev with an oxygen cannula under her nose and three IVs—two dripping into the vein in her left arm and one into her right. She looked so frail that Kvachkov shook his head upon seeing her, sensing that she was long past interrogating and would soon be dead.

"Where's her husband?" the colonel asked, continuing to look at the woman.

"In the room next door."

"Is he in the same physical condition?"

"No. Apparently, he had only limited contact with his sons." Uglov turned slightly to his left to face Kvachkov directly. "The only reason that I called Moscow was to get the chelates. Now I can see that the promise of the medications was only to gain my cooperation with your investigation."

Kvachkov ignored what he'd heard. "I'm going to speak with the husband alone and come back here when I'm through. Just remember, you did Moscow a favor by calling our attention to this problem. We're technically in your debt.

You have some idea of whom I work for. Stay a friend because you also must know how we deal with those who aren't."

Leaving Uglov and the dying woman, Kvachkov went into the adjacent room and found Miras Aliyev lying in bed with a single IV in each arm. Although his face was drawn and morose, he looked like he had a bout of flu rather than an encounter with a deadly radioactive substance.

"I'd like to speak to you about what happened to your wife and children," Kvachkov said, giving the impression that he was a doctor as he walked to the side of the man's bed.

"Is my wife dead?"

"Not yet, but she soon will be. I'm sure you already knew that."

Miras said that he did.

"Tell me what killed your family."

"I don't know. I was inside our residence when my wife yelled for me to come outside, where I saw my sons lying on the ground. While my wife tried to revive them, I ran to the car. Once our sons were inside, my wife continued to try to save them while I drove here as fast as I could."

"Did your sons recently travel anywhere?"

"No. They stay near the house and help with chores. One of them sometimes accompanies me on my weekly trip to Aqtau to get supplies while the other stays and helps their mother. However, neither boy accompanied me this past week."

Kvachkov was an experienced interrogator who could discern from a person's eye movements, posture, tone, facial movements, and other indicators if the person was lying. The fact that Aliyev constantly fidgeted and wouldn't look at Kvachkov directly told him that the man was holding something back.

"What were your children doing just before your wife found them?"

Aliyev's eyes narrowed, and he licked his lips. "I'm tired now. I need to get some rest." The man closed his eyes, hoping to be left alone.

Kvachkov reached down and grabbed the man's throat with both hands so that his airway was barely open. He then pulled his face to within an inch of his. "I may have forgotten to mention that I'm not a doctor and that I work for an organization that's very concerned about what your boys got into. Now, we can do this the easy way, in which you tell me what you know, or the hard way, in which I inflict a great deal of pain before you tell me what you know. Your choice."

The man, who was close to passing out from lack of air, signaled for Kvachkov to release him. Once that happened, he took in several gasps of air, after which he began to speak in a coarse voice. "My sons were stealing from cargo trucks parked at the refueling pump beside the small market we have in our residence."

"And what where those trucks carrying?"

"I don't know because my sons didn't require supervision when they were stealing."

"But you must have taught them what to look for."

"The obvious—alcohol, cigarettes, packaged food, and such that I could sell in my market."

"And you never saw the truck they entered?"

"As I said, I was inside the residence when this happened."

Kvachkov thought for a moment. "Where do you keep what they've stolen?"

"In the basement."

"And did you place the stolen goods there the night they died?"

"No, because I was concerned with my boys and not what they'd taken."

"Did they actually steal something?"

"I don't know. I was only looking at my sons lying on the ground."

"Is someone running your business while you're here?"

"My brother and his wife. I called them."

"And you have no idea what caused your sons' death?"

"I swear."

"I believe you," Kvachkov said as he suddenly pulled the pillow from under the man's head and held it tightly over his face.

Aliyev thrashed wildly and grabbed at Kvachkov's arms as he began to suffocate, but his efforts gradually decreased until there was no movement at all. Kvachkov then put the pillow back under the man's head and pulled the blanket over his body. He returned to the mother's room just as Uglov was pulling the top sheet over her.

"The father just passed away. Cremate the four bodies and delete their records from the hospital's computer system, along with any notes or other records that exist. Everything is to be destroyed."

"I understand," Uglov replied meekly, understanding instinctively that Kvachkov had killed the father.

"I hope you do, because I'm very intolerant of those who don't."

CHAPTER 8

P ARKER MCINNES WAS a four-star army general and
director of the National Security Agency, which was
part of the Department of Defense but operated under
the authority of the DNI—the director of national intelligence.
He was an even six feet tall, had piercing hazel eyes, and was
technically bald; he had some hair on the sides of his head,
but he shaved it daily to maintain a uniform baldness. His
face was chiseled, his jaw was square, and there was very
little fat on his athletic frame. He had managed to retain
his thick chest and muscular appearance from his days as a
linebacker at West Point, largely due to a strenuous two-hour-
a-day exercise regimen. Third-generation army, he was the
son of a retired one-star who had spent his career in military
intelligence and the grandson of a retired colonel who had
held similar positions when he served.

The subject matter of the call that McInnes had just
received from Libby Parra had caught him by surprise. While
Parra waited on the phone, he punched the reference number
that she had given him into the NSA database and slowly
and methodically read the translated conversation between
the doctor in Aqtau, Kazakhstan, and the person he was
trying to convince to send him medicine from Moscow to

treat polonium-210 poisoning. As he read the beginning of the transcript, McInnes was initially skeptical that someone who was essentially a backwater doctor had determined from postmortem tests on two boys that this synthetically produced radioactive substance was the cause of their deaths, but he was a believer by the time he finished.

"This doctor not only had previous experience with polonium-210 poisoning; he also ran instrumented tests at the local university to confirm it. I'm convinced," said McInnes.

"What are the Russians doing with a substance that, according to Google, is 250 billion times more toxic than hydrogen cyanide?" Parra asked.

"As far as we know, the Russians have never produced or stored polonium-210 in Kazakhstan, which makes sense since it's a separate country. And as far as we know, no one in that nation is a particularly big thorn in the side of Vladimir Putin—at least not enough to warrant killing them in a manner that could garner a great deal of publicity if polonium-210 was confirmed as the cause of death," McInnes said.

"Which probably means that the two boys encountered the substance by accident."

"That seems to be a good working theory. I'll forward your intercept to the DNI and the CIA and let them run with it." McInnes ended their conversation by telling Parra that it had been some time since they'd last spoken but that, with Putin's aggressive stance in the world of geopolitics, he believed they'd speak again soon. That prediction would prove to be entirely accurate.

McInnes spent the next hour in and out of three meetings and was about to leave his office for the fourth when he received a second call from Libby Parra on his office phone, along with a simultaneous fax. Their conversation lasted ten minutes, after which he asked his assistant to conference him with both Secretary of Defense James Rosen and the director of national intelligence, Thomas Winegar. Following that call, the DNI asked for a meeting of the National Security Council along with the council's regular attendees and advisors.

The president was the last to arrive in the Situation Room, having walked from the South Lawn after Marine One's arrival from Camp David. He was casually dressed, wearing a slate-gray long-sleeved chamois shirt, khaki slacks, and raisin-colored L.L. Bean Allagash Bison oxford shoes. Once he took his seat at the head of the conference table, everyone sat. In front of each person was a folder containing a translation of the intercept from the NSA SIGINT satellite that had recorded the conversation between King Turki bin Abdulaziz Al Saud of Saudi Arabia and Russian president Vladimir Putin, along with the photograph that had been faxed to McInnes from Parra.

Everyone at the table was silent as they read the intercept. In this call, the king had disclosed to Putin the conversation and the photograph that his country had intercepted between Awalmir Afridi, who was in Peshawar, Pakistan, and a Chechen residing in Grozny, Russia, whose name wasn't mentioned.

The president had received this information earlier in the day and had spoken to President Liu of China, who had been similarly contacted by the king. He now waited patiently for everyone to finish reading.

"That asshole is still alive!" General Robert Trowbridge, chairman of the Joint Chiefs of Staff, loudly remarked, reading about Afridi.

"Apparently," McInnes responded.

After giving everyone another five minutes, the president cleared his throat. Once he had the attention of those around him, he said, "As you can see, Awalmir Afridi has obtained two Soviet-era nuclear weapons and intends to detonate them within China. I have little doubt that this is his way of paying back China—and indirectly us since we're China's largest trading partner—for trying to kill him following the abduction of President Liu and me."

"If the weapons were manufactured by the Soviets," Director Winegar said, "they're very old and could be unstable as internal components deteriorate. Still, we must assume that they've been properly maintained and that both are functional."

"I agree," Secretary of Defense Rosen added. "I suspect that the king sent this photo to enable Putin to research the serial numbers on the weapons and verify that they came from the Soviet Union—hence the courtesy call, if that's what you want to call it."

"Ever since I received this information, I've tried to find a reason that would prompt the king to phone his Russian counterpart rather than have the Saudi ambassador deliver the news to his own counterpart," said McInnes. "Then I realized that this call only made sense if someone in the royal family was involved in the purchase or delivery of the weapons."

The president gave him a quizzical look and said, "Explain that to me."

"Yes, sir. As I said, the king easily could have relayed this information through diplomatic channels. Instead, he erroneously told Putin that his country could listen in on telephone conversations in Pakistan."

"They can't?" the president asked.

"No, sir," McInnes replied. "They don't have that capability. Since the UAE, Oman, and the Arabian Sea separate Saudi Arabia from Pakistan, the Saudis would need to conduct such surveillance from a space-based platform—in other words, a satellite. They currently have three types of satellites in orbit. The Arabsat and the SaudiGeoSat were both built by Lockheed Martin. Therefore, we have the engineering drawings, and neither indicates a monitoring capability. The third type of satellite, the SaudiComsat, is a series of twenty-five-pound nanosatellites. We can't even get our monitoring equipment into an orbital that small."

"So you believe the king wants Putin to recover the nuclear devices because if they're detonated, a full-blown investigation might reveal that a member of the royal family was working with Afridi."

"That's about the size of it, Mr. President. Putin probably knows that Saudi Arabia can't monitor Pakistan's communications. However, he realizes that the origin of the information isn't important, only the information itself. He can't afford for two nuclear weapons manufactured in what's now the Russian Federation to detonate on foreign soil. If that happened, the world community wouldn't believe that he's in control of his nuclear arsenal. Subsequently, they'd hold Russia responsible for the consequences of any detonations," McInnes said.

"As you know," President Ballinger stated while looking at McInnes, "you sent this information to me while I was at Camp David. What you don't know is that I found out from President Liu that King Turki bin Abdulaziz Al Saud phoned and gave him this same song and dance."

"He's covering his bases," Winegar replied.

"That's what I believe. However, it's important to note that since the United States isn't a target, our only involvement will be to continue to monitor the situation. This also goes for the CIA and all the other alphabet agencies," Ballinger said, looking directly at his DNI. "I don't want us even peripherally involved."

"Can I ask why?" Secretary of State Daniel Crenshaw asked.

"A sensible question," the president responded. "Because if we help China, and in the process the bombs explode, the Chinese leadership might accuse us of impeding the disarming of the weapons by giving them false intelligence, or anything else they can think of, so that the people don't blame them but blame their country's largest economic rival instead. The same could be said if we assist Russia. Putin will shed as much blame as he can onto us. As far as the Russians are concerned, the more obfuscation, the better. That's why we're not going to help either the Chinese or them. Get the point? We'd become a convenient scapegoat for both countries."

Crenshaw and most others at the table nodded their heads in agreement.

The meeting adjourned, and after shaking hands with those in attendance, the president left the Situation Room. He went straight to his residence to meet with the passenger who'd accompanied him from Camp David, someone to whom he was about to give orders that would directly contradict the comments he'd just made.

The organization was called Nemesis, named for the Greek goddess of retribution. It had been formed only recently by President Ballinger and President Liu after both leaders were kidnapped and came within a hair of being beheaded, before being found and rescued by a small group of individuals who had acted outside the bureaucracy of Washington and Beijing. Answerable only to the leaders of both nations, Nemesis would be tasked with secretly and aggressively going after those who would do harm to either nation, since both countries faced common enemies and were economically bound at the hip.

Its new headquarters was located within the 716-acre Raven Rock Mountain Complex, which most referred to as Site R, a six-story underground, hardened, self-contained series of structures that were buried deep within the mountain. Functionally, Site R was designed to be the military's backup to the Pentagon in the event of an emergency. As such, it had a twenty-year water supply, power-generation equipment, massive communications capabilities, food storage compartments, and everything else necessary to make it completely self-sufficient. Conveniently, there was a series of tunnels connecting it to Camp David, which was six miles away, as well as to the Pentagon and the NSA. The operational and support staff of Nemesis was kept intentionally small to protect its secrecy. It consisted of a commander, five operatives, and four support staff. Two of those who had a support function, Gao Hui and General Chien An, resided in Beijing, China. Outside these ten people, only the presidents of the United States and China knew of the organization's existence.

Prior to the president's meeting with the National Security Council, the members of Nemesis who were stationed in the United States had assembled at Camp David to celebrate the organization's launch. However, they never got past the meet-and-greet before two calls from President Liu, and one from McInnes, cut the festivities short. The president told Lieutenant Colonel Doug Cray, a former army intelligence officer and the administrative commander of Nemesis, that the team's month-long indoctrination and training schedule was being scrapped. The organization was now operational.

Lieutenant Colonel Cray was in the Solarium as President Ballinger entered the room, having just concluded his meeting. Cray stood as the president approached and was quickly told to sit by the commander in chief.

"Is your team on their way?"

"Yes, sir. They were taken by a Marine Corps helicopter to Joint Base Andrews, given flight suits, boots, and helmets, and then strapped into the back seats of F-16B fighters. That aircraft can attain a speed approaching fifteen hundred miles per hour. Therefore, relatively speaking, it shouldn't take them long to get to northern China."

"Their orders?"

"I repeated what you told them at Camp David—to capture or destroy the two nuclear weapons without anyone learning of their existence."

"And any terrorists they encounter?"

"If possible, capture and turn them over to President Liu or the two members of our Nemesis team who reside in China. If not, bury the bodies where they won't be found." Cray was stressed, which didn't go unnoticed by POTUS.

"Problems?"

"Operationally, no. Every member of Nemesis is a pro who doesn't know how to fail. If we engage, we'll recover the nuclear devices and plant the terrorists. Period."

"Then what is it?"

"It's that matter of 'if we engage.' My analysts had to do a fair amount of extrapolation in their programming to predict where these dirtbags will enter China. It remains to be seen if they picked the right border crossing. China is a very large country."

"You're a former intelligence officer. You can't tell me you haven't at one time or another extrapolated to get to a solution—or in plain English, taken a guess."

"Yes, more often than I care to admit. And this is one of those situations because even though polonium-210 isn't a substance found in any nuclear weapon, the coincidence of two children dying from contact with it in Aqtau, Kazakhstan, makes my analysts believe that the terrorists were also transporting this radioactive substance along with the bombs. Therefore, we gave the route from Aqtau to the Chinese border more weight in our analysis than the dozen or more other variables—such as distance from Grozny, speed of transit, local support, ease of crossing, access to fuel depots, and so forth."

"Where in northern China do you think they'll cross?"

"Khorgas. It's close to the Xinjiang Autonomous Region in the northwest, which is heavily Muslim. Therefore, Afridi may very well have sympathizers or followers there. I've sent the team to the closest Chinese base to that crossing, which, as it turns out, isn't all that close."

"You should expect, thanks to the call from the Saudis, that Putin will be sending operatives to China to try to get to these weapons first because there's no way he wants Soviet-era bombs to detonate on Chinese soil. If that were to happen, President Liu told me that he'd cancel the billions in oil and gas contracts that China has with Russia. That would be devastating to the Russian economy and would likely throw them into a recession."

"Then they'll be desperate to find the weapons and prevent the terrorists from detonating them."

"You can count on that. Whoever Putin sends after the weapons will have no morality or qualms about taking a life. If you encounter the Russian operatives, take whatever measures are necessary to protect your team. They're expendable. You're not."

"I understand, sir. If they try anything, they'll wish they'd never run into Nemesis."

CHAPTER 9

I T WAS TEN fifteen at night. Khalifa bin Nayef was parked in front of Abdul-Malik Kasym's home for the second time this week, but now he was carrying a travel bag containing 500,000 USD, compliments of Al Hakim's bank account. He didn't think of himself as an assassin, having killed only once before and then only when his life was threatened. Tonight, however, that was exactly what he was about to become— because Al Dossari had ordered him to murder Kasym and to do it in a manner that would make his death appear natural. To facilitate that result, he'd been given an inhaler containing a chemical substance that, once it entered the lungs, would induce death within thirty seconds and make it appear as if the victim suffered a heart attack. If he couldn't get the inhaler into Kasym's mouth, he was directed to kill him any way he could. No matter what, he wasn't to leave the Chechen's house until he was dead. As Al Dossari had explained, the reason for this was straightforward. If this caretaker was captured by the Russians and interrogated, he'd put a hole in the story that the king had told Putin. Discovery of this deception would mean that the Russians could blackmail the kingdom and receive significant economic and possibly military concessions to keep the Saudi funding of the detonated weapons a secret from the Chinese. Time was of the essence because the king couldn't give Putin the location of the weapons until the Chechen was dead, and the longer it took to provide that information, the more suspicious the Russian leader would get.

Bin Nayef walked to the front of the house and knocked on the door several times. He waited a minute or so and then tried again. Hearing no response, he pounded his fist even harder on the distressed wood. This time he heard a distant voice announce that he was coming and then ask who was there. Using his cover story, bin Nayef responded that he had a delivery from Al Hakim.

Kasym turned on the porch light and slowly opened the door, but only as far as the chain on it would allow. Looking through the narrow opening, bin Nayef saw a handgun aimed at his midsection by a man with a distrusting look on his face.

"I don't know that person, and I'm not expecting a delivery."

"Prince Husam Al Hakim sends his apologies for this intrusion. He told me to say that he will communicate with you tomorrow. I'm only a messenger. If you like, I can put this bag down on the porch and leave."

"What's in it?"

"Money."

"How do I know it isn't a bomb?"

Nayef opened the bag and dumped the bundles of cash on the front porch. The old man's face displayed surprise, and his eyes darted from side to side, as if he was checking to see if any of his neighbors were around.

"Pick up the money and put it back in the bag, quickly," he said, closing the door and releasing the chain. The door reopened just as bin Nayef had finished placing the last of the bundles of cash back into the bag and was zipping it shut. Kasym was still holding his gun at waist level.

"Please take this, and I'll be on my way," bin Nayef said, extending the heavy bag to the old man, who moved his gun aside to accept it.

In the blink of an eye, bin Nayef grabbed the old man, spun him around, and put his left arm tightly around his throat. Kasym lost his grip on the gun, and it dropped to the floor. With Kasym gasping for breath, bin Nayef took the inhaler out of his pocket, shoved it into the man's mouth, and squeezed. Half a minute later, Kasym's body jerked several times and then went limp.

Taking a pair of latex gloves out of his jacket pocket, the investigator began searching the 1,200-square-foot residence, but after forty-five minutes he had found nothing of interest. With only one other item on his agenda, he walked out the back door and went to the garage to make certain that nothing there or in the chamber with the weapons could incriminate a member of the royal family. Turning on the overhead lights, he used the electric gantry crane to move aside the large steel plates, after which he searched for and found the light switch for the underground chamber to the side of the ladder. When he looked down into the chamber, the shock of what he saw—or more accurately, what he didn't see—caused his legs to buckle, and he fell onto his knees. The bombs were gone.

Most of China's ten and a half million Muslims lived in the Xinjiang Autonomous Region in the northwest part of the country, which lay adjacent to Kazakhstan. Here the border city of Khorgas, once a remote outpost, had evolved into a key ground-transport gateway for Chinese goods to enter Kazakhstan and to be driven from there to Europe, which was cheaper than transport by rail or ship. However, this trade was largely one-way because there was little demand for European goods within the Xinjiang Autonomous Region. As a result, the trucks going in the opposite direction, from Kazakhstan to China, were largely empty.

It was within this group of cargoless carriers that the two M35s waited to cross into China. The night before, Samara had gotten rid of all the contraband that both vehicles carried, believing that trying to enter China with illicit goods might invite a very thorough search because the Chinese were said to have zero tolerance for smugglers. This supposition seemed to be verified by the two VT-5 light combat tanks parked adjacent to the inspection station and the multitude of People's Liberation Army soldiers inspecting vehicles and patrolling the area.

When Samara's truck reached the front of the line, an inspector directed it to park on a large rectangular metal plate where it would be weighed. Once it was on the scale, chocks were placed in front of and behind the front wheels, preventing the truck from leaving until the inspectors were through. The other M35 was undergoing a similar process at a parallel inspection station.

Samara watched as six inspectors, three to a truck, unloaded bags of concrete and other construction materials and laid them flat on the ground. They randomly cut open several of the bags, looking for anything that might be concealed within. Finding no contraband, one of them stepped into the vehicle closest to Samara and apparently saw something at the far end. He walked through the truck to the wooden panel behind the cab and ran his hand over two screws that were protruding slightly from the panel.

Removing a small screwdriver from his jacket pocket, he began to remove the panel.

Samara's eyes widened, and he started toward the inspector but stopped after only a step—with two tanks and a score of armed PLA soldiers not far from the vehicle, there was nothing he could do to stop the intrusion. The inspector had just removed the second protruding screw when Samara heard someone behind him yelling in Chinese.

Turning, Samara saw a short squat man with black-rimmed glasses. He was probably a senior noncommissioned officer, judging from his demeanor and the three fat chevrons on the epaulet of his uniform, and he was shouting at the inspectors, each of whom displayed a rank of one thin chevron. The NCO pointed to the long line of vehicles behind him and threw up his arms in apparent exasperation that the two vehicles, which carried no contraband, weren't being reloaded with their construction materials and sent on their way. Since PLA NCOs weren't criticized for breaching political correctness or being insensitive in their speech or actions to those of lesser rank, the six inspectors helped reload the trucks in record time. Ten minutes after the NCO barked his orders, the two M35s exited the inspection station and entered Khorgas.

Once they were through the Chinese border crossing, Samara wanted to stop in Khorgas to refuel the trucks. Also wanting to see if Afridi had sent him a message, he found a gas station with an internet café nearby and went inside the café while his men were refueling the vehicles. Buying time on one of the machines in the corner, Samara accessed the internet address that Afridi had given him and found two messages. He opened the first message and converted the gibberish that appeared on his screen using one of the OTPs that he'd been given. Once he had finished reading, he started taking deep breaths to control his anxiety.

According to Afridi, contact with both Kasym and Al Hakim had been lost. They'd previously been on a strict communication schedule, which had been flawlessly followed until three days ago, when both failed to check in. Therefore, Afridi suspected that they'd both been compromised. The second message, which Samara decrypted using a second OTP, was something that he expected, given that two members of their inner circle had gone silent. After acknowledging the receipt of both messages, he ended his session and walked outside. Taking a lighter from his pocket, he burned both OTPs on which he'd translated the messages, then crushed their ashes with his boot. He then returned to the gas station, where he found his men waiting beside their trucks.

"There's been a change of plans," Samara said as he approached.

Colonel Vasily Kvachkov had been to the Kremlin many times, but never to see Vladimir Putin. His chauffeured Mercedes S560 arrived at the entrance to the Kremlin thirty minutes before his 8:00 a.m. meeting, and after his identification and appointment with the president were confirmed, and the interior and underside of his vehicle were inspected for bombs and sniffed by a German shepherd, the vehicle was allowed to enter. It then proceeded to the old Senate building, where Putin kept his office. The three-story neoclassical structure, which was painted the same yellow as many of the other buildings within the Kremlin, was shaped like an isosceles triangle, each side 330 feet in length. It was adjacent to the Kremlin Wall, and one side paralleled Red Square.

As Kvachkov stepped from his vehicle, he saw a silver Mi-8 military helicopter land on the helipad fifty yards in front of him. Waiting around the periphery of the landing zone were six security personnel, each wearing a black suit, white shirt, and black tie. As soon as the wheels hit the ground, they approached the aircraft door. They surrounded Putin as he stepped out and walked to the side entrance of the building.

Kvachkov went to the visitor's door, which was on the same side of the building but one hundred feet away from the entrance that Putin had used. Entering the nondescript lobby, he presented his military ID to the guard stationed at the entrance, who verified that he was expected and directed him to the x-ray machine and metal and explosives detector. After he passed through both scanners, he was given a full-body pat-down, after which he was approached by one of the security staff and escorted to the third-floor waiting room outside Putin's office.

The walls of the fifty-by-fifty-foot waiting space were light blue, interrupted at intervals by stark white columns. The hardwood floor was arranged in an intricate herringbone pattern and was worn but highly polished. Security was limited to two guards on either side of the double doors through which Kvachkov had entered, as well as another two who were standing next to the doors that led into the president's office. Each wore crisp black military fatigues and was armed with an automatic rifle and a handgun.

The FSB colonel did not get an opportunity to sit in one of the dozen blue-cushioned waiting room chairs because as soon as his escort gave his name to Putin's administrative assistant, an attractive and efficient-looking five foot ten blonde in her early forties with shoulder-length hair, she immediately escorted him into the president's office.

Putin was sitting behind a large antique desk centered in the back of his 1,500-square-foot office, talking on the phone. With a nod to his assistant, the president of the Russian Federation silently pointed to a small circular table beside a white marbled fireplace at the back of his office.

Kvachkov had been told by his superiors that Putin didn't chitchat, disliked those who did, and distrusted anyone who appeared weak, smiled too much, or continually agreed with his point of view. Instead, he expected to hear what someone really thought. Different points of view were encouraged. However, once the Russian strongman decided, everyone was expected to fall in line.

Putin finished his phone call and walked to Kvachkov, the FSB colonel coming to attention as the president approached. After both men took their seats, Putin complimented Kvachkov for cleaning up the situation regarding the polonium-210 deaths in Aqtau.

Smiling at the praise given to him by the most powerful person in the country, the colonel barely had a chance to savor the compliment before Putin told him that he was being given another assignment that, if successful, would result in his promotion to the rank of major general.

"I don't fail," Kvachkov responded.

"Your personnel file indicates as much."

"What's my assignment?" Kvachkov asked with enthusiasm.

"Recover two Soviet-era nuclear weapons that are being, or already have been, smuggled into China by associates of the terrorist Awalmir Afridi, who are intent upon detonating them somewhere within the country."

In a matter of seconds, the colonel's facial expression changed from one of gratitude for what he had felt was his assured promotion to one of anticipation over what he would be asked to do to one of concentration as he listened to Putin describe his mission and finally to one of realization that the mission would take place inside China.

"This came as a surprise to all of us," Putin said, apparently reading at least some of Kvachkov's expressions. "The stark reality is that if these weapons are detonated on Chinese soil, President Liu will hold Russia just as responsible as Afridi for our failure to keep our nuclear weapons out of the hands of terrorists."

"Do we have any idea where the weapons are?"

"Intelligence believes that the polonium-210 that you encountered in Aqtau is on the same transport vehicles as these weapons. It's too big a coincidence for it not to be. However, even if it's not, our people have indicated that the only practical way to take these weapons from Aqtau to China and avoid the rigorous inspection and detection measures employed in Chinese mass transit terminals would be to put them in a truck. One could then drive the devices across Kazakhstan and into northwestern China and from there transport them anywhere."

"But we don't know if the nuclear devices have crossed the border into China?"

"Undetermined." As he spoke, Putin opened the bottle of Five Lakes vodka that sat in the center of the table, then poured each of them a shot glass of the Siberian-made drink.

"Vashe zdorovie," the president said, wishing him good health before downing his drink.

Kvachkov followed suit and drained his glass. "How do I find the weapons?" he asked.

"We have equipment that can locate them, even if the weapons are enclosed within six feet of solid steel."

"Really?" Kvachkov exclaimed involuntarily.

"I was a skeptic at first, but a field demonstration of this device changed my mind. Are you familiar with muons?"

"No," Kvachkov admitted.

"Neither was I before I was educated on them. I'm told a muon is cosmic radiation that penetrates all matter without interacting with it. However, when the particles hit heavy elements like uranium, they deflect. Our sensors detect this deflection and construct a 3-D image of the shape of the object they hit. We can therefore look for these nuclear weapons by searching for the deflection of muons," Putin said.

"When do I get started?"

"Today," Putin answered as he poured two more drinks. "Za milyh dam," he said, toasting beautiful women before throwing the shot down his throat.

Kvachkov followed and downed the smooth Siberian vodka in one gulp.

"Your driver will take you to FSB headquarters. Select your men and have our overseas department issue visas and get your airline tickets to Urumqi, China, which is in the northwestern part of the country. After that, you're on your own. It goes without saying that you and your men are ghosts and don't exist as far as my government is concerned."

"I don't fail, Mr. President."

"Then *uspeshnost*," Putin said, refilling their glasses.

"Success," Kvachkov repeated in Russian.

CHAPTER 10

U S SENATOR RUFUS Lynn went to the bar at the rear of his office, poured three fingers of scotch into a crystal tumbler, and then lowered his pudgy six foot two, 330-pound frame into the La-Z-Boy adjacent to the bar and beside his desk. With his free hand he pulled back on the reclining lever just enough to take the weight off his feet, but not so far as to make it difficult for him to down the thirty-year-old Balvenie scotch extracted from the case one of his constituents sent to him monthly.

Named after Rufus King, a Massachusetts lawyer who had signed the Constitution, the four-term Democratic senator was vice chairman of the Senate Select Committee on Intelligence. The media consensus was that in the next general election, he'd be the Democratic flag bearer for the nation's highest office. However, the polls also showed that President Ballinger would crush anyone running against him. Consequently, Lynn's advisors had emphasized that if he was to be a viable candidate, he needed something that would permanently tarnish the conservative president's reputation and turn the country against him. The problem with that idea was that POTUS was a Boy Scout who had no skeletons in his closet. In the world of Washington politics, that was unheard of. Therefore, Lynn constantly put out feelers to members of his party, as well as lobbyists and government officials who had a vested interest in his success, for anything that would put a dent in Ballinger's persona. If the Boy Scout image held up into November, the upcoming election would be a replay of Humphrey and Goldwater's run for the White House.

This morning, at an intelligence briefing given by Secretary of Defense James Rosen, his bullshit meter had gone into overdrive when Rosen told him that the president had established an analytical group, known as the White House Statistical Analysis Division, that would report directly to him. Furthermore, it was to be headquartered at Site R in the emergency relocation space previously designated for the Senate Select Committee on Intelligence. What bothered Lynn was that this was the first time, in a city that held its secrets as well as a sieve held water, that he was hearing about this new analytical group. He questioned why the president needed it since he received a daily briefing from the director of national intelligence that fused together data from every component of the intelligence community. Lynn had seen the presidential brief many times, and it was information overload. Why then would POTUS need to analyze anything on his own? If he had a question, the DNI could task the relevant agency with getting the intelligence on whatever the president requested. Therefore, Ballinger had established this division for a purpose other than analysis, and with a score of people who owed him a favor, Rufus Lynn was going to find out exactly what that purpose was.

In Washington it was widely accepted that the truth was variable depending on one's objective. Everyone knew and followed that assumption because it was considered an axiom of politics. Taking a long pull on his scotch, the senator pondered whether the Boy Scout had adopted this philosophy with his establishment of the White House Statistical Analysis Division.

Getting up from the La-Z-Boy, he refreshed his glass of scotch and removed a nine-and-a-quarter-inch Cuban Montecristo A, which the British ambassador regularly provided, from the humidor on his desk. After biting off the end and spitting it into his trash can, he took a lighter from his pocket and lit the cigar until he had an even ash. Although it was nine in the morning, the combination of the cigar and brown water, as he liked to refer to scotch, always helped him think clearly.

Thirty minutes later, halfway through the Montecristo, the answer came when he realized that a common access card, referred to as a CAC by the military, was needed for entry not only into Site R but also into the space this new division occupied within the complex. Each digitized card contained an integrated circuit chip, a unique PIN, and a color photo of the cardholder. Therefore, whoever had been assigned to this sham analytical function would need one. The problem was getting this information without creating suspicion.

Reaching into his right pants pocket, he pulled out his cell phone, looked up a name on his contact list, and called Colonel Jonathan Brass, commander of the Raven Rock Mountain Complex. As vice chairman of the Senate Select Committee on Intelligence and a rumored presidential candidate, Lynn believed he had what those in Washington called "juice," meaning enough power to force someone to do something as an accommodation. Therefore, after exchanging small talk with Brass, he told the colonel that he needed the video for the security camera facing the former offices used by his committee. The reason, he claimed, was that as a potential presidential candidate, he needed to prove that he'd attended committee meetings at Site R and didn't sit on his lazy ass in Washington—the latter of which was closer to the truth. Lynn told Brass that he couldn't recall the exact dates of the meetings he'd attended, but if the colonel could provide the security feeds for the past month, that would suffice.

Brass listened patiently to the senator's request without comment, then stated that such a decision was above his pay grade and that he would need authorization from someone higher up in his chain of command before he could release the videos.

After Brass hung up with the good senator from Illinois, he called his boss at the Pentagon, a brigadier general, and relayed Lynn's request.

"The video feeds aren't classified," the colonel said, "but the period requested is overly broad. The system will give us exactly when the senator entered that office space, and I could provide him with just that visual surveillance rather than an entire month."

"What I'm more concerned about," said the brigadier general, "is the documentation of lack of attendance by other members of the Senate Select Committee on Intelligence. In my experience, those in Congress are always leery of their constituents knowing how many meetings they missed."

"Point taken."

"However, if lightning strikes, he could become president. Lynn's not known for playing nice and I'm sure he has friends, on the Appropriations Committee and in the Pentagon, who'd make an example of us just to get a favor from him. Therefore, if he wants to see the surveillance feed for the last month, then give it to him. However, when you send it, make sure he signs a receipt and agrees that the surveillance footage is not to be released to the public. That way we'll cover our asses."

"I'll draw up the hand receipt now," the colonel said before ending the call.

Phoning Lynn, Brass relayed the conditions that the brigadier general had given him, and Lynn replied that the terms were acceptable. After the phone call ended, Brass had the master sergeant in charge of the complex's video surveillance system retrieve the requested footage, and two hours later, a flash drive with the requested video data was in the hands of a military courier.

The Honorable Senator Rufus Lynn was reclined in his La-Z-Boy and had just finished a glass of brown water and was in the process of pouring himself another when he heard a knock on his office door. Opening it, he saw an army captain who immediately saluted and handed him a flash drive, along with a delivery receipt and a pen.

Not bothering to read what he was signing, Lynn returned the receipt to the officer and sent him away with an imperious wave of his hand. Taking the flash drive to his desktop computer, after a detour to get his glass of scotch, he inserted it and fast-forwarded until he saw an army lieutenant colonel, whose name tag read "Cray," and a Secret Service agent, whom he'd previously seen guarding the president, enter the space formerly used by his committee. In the following weeks both men came and went, along with groups of civilians who were delivering and probably installing racks of electronic equipment. Two young civilians, men in their twenties, joined the Secret Service agent and army officer as regulars, entering and leaving at all times of the day and night.

Lynn rubbed his bloodshot eyes, took a long swallow of brown water, and continued reviewing the digital recording. The video surveillance from the previous day showed four other individuals, two of Asian descent, also entering the analytical division's space. Zooming in, he copied all eight individuals' facial images onto his hard drive. He couldn't ask Brass for their names, although the CAC each used would immediately provide their identities, because that request wouldn't correlate with the story that he'd concocted. He'd need another source, an agency with an outrageously big facial database, to uncover their identities.

Thinking on it, Lynn narrowed his options down to the FBI and the DOD, both of which had the required databases and, more importantly, people who owed him favors. The Department of Homeland Security would have been a better choice because it had the largest facial recognition database, but Secretary Mike Zvanovec was a stickler for the rules and would want a formal request and legal justification before conducting such a search. He was also a Ballinger loyalist, which meant that seconds after Lynn made the request, Zvanovec would be on the phone to POTUS. Therefore, DHS wasn't a consideration.

Lynn decided to start with his contact at the FBI, given that the DOD might become curious since he'd just asked them for the surveillance videos. He emailed his request to the person who owed him the favor and attached the images of the eight individuals who he believed worked in what the president purported to be his analytical division.

It was five in the morning when Lynn was awoken from a deep sleep by the warbling tone of an incoming fax. Groggy, he slowly brought the back and footrest of the La-Z-Boy forward and lifted his large frame off the chair, stumbling slightly because he was still half-asleep and hungover. The fax machine, which was on the right edge of his desk and several feet from him, was spitting out paper as he walked toward it. Once it finished, Lynn grabbed the eight pages from the tray and returned to his La-Z-Boy.

His FBI contact had been able to identify the eight individuals and had provided not only each person's name but also summary background information. The two geeks were Michael Connelly and Kyle Alexson, former NSA analysts. Lieutenant Colonel Douglas Cray, Major Peter Cancelliere, and a civilian named Matthew Moretti all worked for the US Army Intelligence and Security Command. The Asian woman was Han Li, identified from a flight she'd made from China to Joint Base Andrews. The other Asian was Lieutenant Colonel Yan He of the People's Liberation Army, a former aide to the chief of the general staff of the People's Liberation Army. The last page contained the picture and summary bio of former Secret Service agent Jack Bonaquist.

"Why would Ballinger grant two Chinese citizens access to one of the United States' most sensitive installations?" Lynn muttered to himself. "And what are they doing working with army intelligence without my committee, or seemingly anyone else in the government, knowing about it? The Boy Scout is about to have his wings clipped."

Lynn, who had been continually reelected to the Senate because he was a savvier political strategist than his opponents, started to dial his friend at the *Washington Post* to give him this information on the Boy Scout. However, just before he pressed the last digit on his cell phone, he stopped.

"You're being stupid, Rufus," he said. "If this information gets out, every Democrat in Congress will compete for the nomination because they'll see Ballinger as vulnerable. Keep this to yourself until after the DNC convention and keep probing into what the Boy Scout is up to."

The Honorable Rufus Lynn decided to heed his own advice.

CHAPTER 11

T HE FIVE AIR Force F-16B Falcon aircraft, the combat-capable training version of the otherwise single-seat fighter, had flown 6,753 miles, had refueled in the air a number of times, and were now on final approach to a Soviet-era air base in northwest China. Matt Moretti, Han Li, Peter Cancelliere, Jack Bonaquist, and Yan He were in the back seats of these aircraft as they set down on the 8,000-foot-long runway and then taxied toward a cluster of weathered buildings and hangars that dated back to the early 1960s.

The F-16s were directed by the tower to park behind a row of two dozen J-11 fighter aircraft and beside two large helicopters, each resembling the US military's Black Hawk. Once their engines were shut down and canopies opened, a battered Chinese vehicle, resembling a 1950s-era jeep, pulled behind the five aircraft. A military officer opened the vehicle's creaky passenger door and stepped onto the tarmac, then waited for the crew and passengers to deplane. As the members of the Nemesis team, wearing green flight suits without insignias or name tags, removed their helmets and stepped onto terra firma, the officer looked at each face and compared it with an image that he'd memorized.

"Lieutenant Colonel He?" the officer asked as he approached the last person to deplane.

After Yan He nodded in the affirmative, the officer gave him a crisp salute and handed over the ten-by-thirteen-inch manila envelope he carried in his right hand. A brief conversation ensued, after which the officer returned to his vehicle and left.

"What was that about?" Moretti asked as he and the other team members approached Yan He.

"President Liu sent him from Beijing to deliver this envelope to us," the lieutenant colonel said, holding up what had been handed to him. "Let's go inside and open it."

Yan He led the way into the base operations building behind them, a one-story unpainted concrete structure beside a thirty-foot flagpole whose Chinese flag was snapping in the wind. Once in the building, they found a small conference room to the right of the entrance. Yan He opened the envelope and removed its contents: two groups of photos, each bound together with a small binder clip, a rectangular piece of paper with Chinese writing on it, and a folded map.

Yan He read the message and then summarized it. "Yesterday, our border security system detected these two trucks entering China at the Khorgas border crossing," he said, unclipping the first set of photos and placing them side by side on the conference table, which was eight feet long and four feet wide. Although there were wooden straight-backed chairs around the table, everyone stood as they took in the message from President Liu. The photos provided frontal views of two M35 trucks, and each bore a date and time stamp in the lower right corner.

"The government office in Khorgas put the license plate numbers on these two vehicles into our national transportation database, whereby they were found to be forged. Unfortunately, the computer system at the crossing is old, slow, and badly in need of updating. In addition, no priority was given to this database search. Therefore, it took ten hours before the local government received word that the plates were forged. The president can't unring that bell, but he has ordered a nationwide priority search for these trucks. However, there's a complication."

"There always is," Moretti said, not in the tone of a smart ass, but as a professional among other professionals acknowledging that nothing was ever easy or straightforward in their line of work.

"Exactly. The problem is that these vehicles may have taken one of the many back roads in this area, where camera surveillance doesn't exist. While on these roads, they'd be almost impossible to find."

The two photographs of the M35 trucks, with their license plates clearly visible, were making their way around the table.

"In addition to photographing the license plates, we were also able to obtain photos of the drivers and passengers." Yan He unclipped the second group of photos, which zoomed in on the two drivers and those sitting next to them. He handed the headshots of the five men, who appeared to be of Middle Eastern descent, to Moretti.

Moretti looked through the photos before sending them around the table. "They could be anywhere by now," he said.

"I agree. But if they intend to detonate these weapons, sooner or later they'll need to take a major highway to reach a populated area. Back roads in China generally don't go far, and they're mostly in rural areas because local governments, rather than the national government, fund, construct, and maintain them. Therefore, when these men drive on a major highway, which all have camera surveillance, we'll know exactly where they are," Yan He said.

"Do you believe they're targeting Beijing and Shanghai?" Bonaquist asked Yan He.

"That's my assumption. However, these terrorists will never make it anywhere near either city because in addition to camera surveillance, all highways leading to major urban centers have radiation sensors."

"Then what's our next step?" Moretti asked. Normally the team leader, Moretti had made it clear before the team boarded the F-16s that the lieutenant colonel would be calling the shots this time because this operation was on Chinese soil.

Yan He unfolded the map, which included the position of surveillance cameras, on the desk. "To get out of the area, they'll eventually have to get on either highway G30, which goes north, or highway G218, which heads south," he said, pointing to both on his map. "The only difference is that the northern route is an expressway, which has both monitoring cameras and weigh scales, while the southern route, at least according to this map, doesn't have either until we get one hundred miles beyond Khorgas."

"We divide into two," Moretti concluded.

"We divide into two teams," Yan He confirmed. "Cancelliere, Bonaquist, and I will take one of the helicopters you saw outside and investigate the northern route, while Moretti and Han Li take the south. The helicopters will allow us to check the back roads as well as the main highways. Two M35 trucks should be relatively easy to spot from the air."

"And once we find them?" Cancelliere asked.

"Eliminate the terrorists with extreme prejudice and recover the weapons."

No one had a problem with that order. Each member of Nemesis had agreed before they left Joint Base Andrews that anyone who intended to set off a nuclear weapon should immediately get his ticket to the afterlife punched. They weren't interested in taking prisoners, giving interrogations, or reading Miranda rights. All they cared about was putting those callous enough to set off these devices into body bags.

"The messenger you saw told me that we have weapons, gear, and communications equipment waiting for us in the helicopters. Let's change and get moving."

Senator Rufus Lynn entered the Capital Grille on Pennsylvania Avenue and looked around. The person he was meeting hadn't yet arrived, so he took a seat at his usual table in the back and ordered a double shot of twenty-five-year-old Macallan's scotch, straight up. The always efficient waitstaff had just brought his beverage when Marshall Beck, assistant secretary of defense for legislative affairs, walked in.

"I'll have an iced tea," Beck said to a waiter standing nearby, before taking a seat opposite Lynn. His usual pattern was to meet with the senator once a month at a time when the lunch crowd had gone, and the restaurant was nearly deserted. Neither came to eat. They were there to talk.

Beck's position within the DOD had a singular focus: maintaining good relationships with Congress. When the Pentagon wanted more money, a new weapons system, or to avoid budget cuts, this was the branch of government they'd have to come to, with hat in hand, in order to get what they wanted—not that the Pentagon didn't have some leverage of its own. Its usual recourse was to threaten the closure of a military installation, which would result in a severe financial impact within a congressional area. When someone spoke about losing votes, Congress listened. Accustomed to this negotiating ritual, and knowing that nothing was free in Washington, both sides attempted to accumulate chits for favors provided and, at the appropriate time, cash them in.

As soon as Beck's iced tea arrived, Lynn told the waiter that they weren't to be disturbed and they'd summon him if they needed anything. The senator then drained the last of the scotch and put down the empty glass between them.

"I have a question for the Department of Defense," Lynn said. "Is the Pentagon planning a joint exercise with the Chinese that you failed to disclose to my committee?"

"Not that I'm aware."

"That's hard to believe because someone told me that they saw a Chinese officer and an Asian woman, who looked Chinese, visiting Site R. In fact, they were seen going into my committee's old digs. If that's true—and you know I wouldn't bring it up if I didn't have proof—would you like to explain to me and my constituents why in the hell the Pentagon would permit Chinese nationals entrance to an installation as sensitive as the Raven Rock Mountain Complex?" Whenever Lynn was feeling self-righteous, he always mentioned his constituents. Otherwise, they were an afterthought to his aspirations of power in Washington.

"You're well informed, as usual, Senator. I just learned about these two individuals yesterday. However, there's no joint exercise. The White House told SecDef that President Liu sent them as liaisons to effectuate better coordination between our militaries. Considering we previously have had no communication channel between our armed forces, which would have been helpful when Presidents Ballinger and Liu were kidnapped, both believed it was time to establish a military backchannel."

"Poppycock. A backchannel involves two parties, and I haven't heard of an American military officer walking into their equivalent of Site R. Moreover, if they're liaisons, why the secrecy and the failure to notify my committee of their arrival? You and your boss are smart enough to know that congressional approval would be needed to fund this venture. The DOD is hiding something. If you're going to pump sunshine up someone's ass, Mr. Assistant Secretary, try one of the gullible first-termers."

Beck took a deep breath and replied in an even and measured tone. "Senator, I can only tell you what the White House has told the DOD."

Lynn looked for the waiter whom he'd prematurely sent away before his glass was topped off with brown water. He was unable to see him, and the abruptness and tone of his next question reflected his irritation at running low on alcohol. "Where are those two Chinese now?"

"They took off from Joint Base Andrews yesterday for China."

"We don't send military aircraft into China, do we?"

"Not until yesterday. The two Chinese nationals, along with three Americans, were placed in the back seats of F-16B aircraft and flown to China."

"Now why in the hell would the DOD do that?"

"Because the president ordered us to get them to their destination as quickly as possible."

"Why wasn't Congress told?"

"The president wanted to keep the Chinese liaisons' presence in the United States and the flights to China on a need-to-know basis. The rumor was that he didn't want to look foolish if negotiations on the backchannel collapsed."

"That's politically reasonable. However, you'd think that the cat would be out of the bag when five American fighters landed in Beijing. Word is bound to get out since Beijing is inland, and any approach, even to a military base, would traverse civilian areas. That's not a very smart play, politically speaking, if the president is trying to keep this under his hat. Putting them on a commercial aircraft would have been smarter—unless he was in an ungodly hurry to get them there, that is."

"They're not going to Beijing. They were flying to a Chinese air base in northwest China, not far from the Kazakhstan border."

"Are you sure?"

"Positive. The flight plans are classified, but you obviously have the clearance and the need-to-know, which is why I'm telling you. The air force provided the pilots and the en route airborne refueling."

"Airborne refueling? Again, why was the president in such a hurry to get them to their destination? If he's establishing a backchannel, which would obviously consider the national security sensitivities of both countries, an agreement of that nature is bound to take some time."

Beck shrugged.

"And what the hell is in northwest China? As far as we know, the Chinese equivalent of Site R isn't anywhere near Kazakhstan." Before Beck could reply, Lynn continued speaking. "It doesn't matter. Inform me immediately if you learn anything more about what we're doing in China because I don't like being kept in the dark." His tone made it clear that there would be repercussions if he was lied to.

"If I learn anything, you'll be informed within minutes."

"I'm counting on it."

Returning to his office, Lynn poured himself a large glass of brown water, pulled a Montecristo A from his humidor, and sat in his La-Z-Boy. Halfway through his cigar, and after his third glass of brown water, he again reviewed the background summaries on those who had entered the new presidential workspace at Site R. That's when the noninebriated portion of his brain came up with an idea, and he called Beck.

Each of the satellite photos that Rufus Lynn had received from Assistant Secretary Marshall Beck, which were now spread across his desk, displayed an impressive level of imagery detail. Together, they gave a much different story from the fairy tale the president was trying to whiff by Congress.

His call to Beck, threatening to hold a public hearing on why US Force F-16B Falcon aircraft were in China, was all it had taken to get photographs from an imagery intelligence or IMINT satellite that was retasked to northwest China. The first photo showed the five people he had seen at Site R entering one of two Chinese Z-20 helicopters. The second photograph had several of them exiting this aircraft and entering the other, wearing what appeared to be black tactical gear not unlike what one would wear on a military operation. In addition, each wore a handgun and carried an automatic weapon. The third photo showed Chinese military pilots, judging from the fact that they were wearing flight suits with rank on their shoulders, entering the helicopters. The fourth and final photo was of both helicopters lifting off.

Rufus Lynn might not be the sharpest pencil in the pack, but he was street-smart. Whatever these five people that POTUS had sent to northwest China were up to, it had nothing to do with establishing a military backchannel.

Instead, it appeared to be about combat, or at least some measure of conflict. How else could the tactical gear and weapons be explained? This wasn't exactly how one dressed at the negotiating table outside Iraq and Afghanistan. Lynn again dialed Beck and this time told him that he needed the IMINT satellite to follow the two helicopters like a hawk.

It had taken Awalmir Afridi several days to drive across Pakistan and reach Manora, a small peninsula south of the Port of Karachi on the Arabian Sea. Connected to the mainland by a seven-and-a-half-mile causeway called the Sandspit, the peninsula's marina berthed nearly a hundred small craft, the largest measuring thirty-four feet, as well as one enormous 183-foot-long Benetti yacht named *The Golden One.* The crew of the vessel, which Al Hakim had loaned to Afridi so that he could ride out the global search for him in the aftermath of the nuclear explosions, were told to take the terrorist leader thirty miles from land and anchor there while a doctor surgically reconstructed his face and changed his fingerprints. The physician and his team, who'd performed similar operations on persons wanted by the US government, were already on board. The first surgery would take place in the morning, with subsequent operations conducted over the course of the year, depending on how fast he healed. In the end, the surgeries would allow Awalmir Afridi to evade detection by facial and fingerprint recognition systems.

The nuclear devices being transported by his cousin would detonate in forty-eight hours, after which China would be economically devastated, and the world's economy and stock markets would come crashing down. Afridi planned to take advantage of this economic chaos by using whatever money remained in the Protectors of Islam bank accounts to short global stock indexes, betting they would come apart at the seams. In two days, he'd become a multibillionaire, and for the rest of his life, he would live the exorbitant lifestyle he deserved.

CHAPTER 12

T HE TWO M35 cargo trucks left the gas station at Khorgas and completed the fifty-mile drive down highway G218 to Yining, a city of 430,000 residents, in a little less than an hour. Khorgas had two primary industries—fruit orchard farming and mining. Therefore, the surrounding area was a stark contrast of large patches of trees on one side of the highway and massive holes in the earth on the other.

The last email that Samara had received from Afridi disclosed Al Hakim's death—supposedly of natural causes, which Afridi did not believe, of course—and the need to change their plans in the event their late benefactor had told the person who interrogated him what he knew about their mission. Although Al Hakim had not been told the details of how the bombs would reach their destinations, Kasym was on his payroll and was a treasure trove of information—he knew the identities on their forged passports, the license plate numbers of their trucks, and other information critical to tracking them. Afridi didn't know whether Kasym also had been interrogated and killed, but if not, the assumption was that he soon would be. Therefore, he had decided to get rid of the trucks one city earlier than intended and use another mode of transportation to transport the weapons. Fortunately, the timing was perfect for that to occur.

Both M35s entered the empty parking lot of the Yining Drilling Supply Company, which occupied a 100,000-square-foot dull yellow rectangular building, and parked to the right of the four-foot-wide concrete walkway leading to the entrance. After directing the other men to remain inside their vehicles, Samara picked up a small soft-sided black suitcase from the floorboard and entered the building. There he was immediately confronted by a salesman, who, after determining that the person he was addressing didn't understand Chinese, summoned his supervisor. Samara and the supervisor were both multilingual, and they eventually found that English was their common language and established a dialogue, not that speech was critical to the transaction. Samara was familiar with the company's website, which had been translated into three languages, and if necessary could have pointed to the two Diamec U8 core drilling rigs that he was there to obtain, one of which was on display just a few feet from where he was standing. The company's website indicated that three were in inventory. However, if they'd been sold already, there were other pieces of equipment that could be purchased instead.

His cover story was that he'd just been awarded contracts in Beijing and Shanghai that commenced the same week, each requiring a Diamec U8 or a rig with similar capabilities. Although this equipment was available in both cities, this type of rig was primarily manufactured in northwest China, where materials, labor, and just about all goods and services were cheaper. Therefore, there was a logic to Samara buying the Diamecs in Yining rather than purchasing them from a reseller in another city, where handling, cartage, and urban markups significantly increased the price.

However, the supervisor couldn't care less about what his customer was going to do with the rigs or how much money he'd save by buying the equipment in Yining. Instead, he was focused on the stacks of cash Samara had removed from his soft-sided suitcase and was likely thinking of the commission he'd receive on the quarter of a million dollars in US currency that was stacked on the table.

The bill of sale required the company name, address, and phone number and a host of other information—all of which was provided and all of which was fictitious. However, since the transaction was in cash, none of these details needed to be verified. Once the paperwork was complete, Samara requested that the equipment be crated for shipment by rail and that the company prepare the transit documents, since these obviously needed to be in Chinese, and pay the transport fees in advance to where the rigs would be sent, the location of which he subsequently provided. Once the cost of these services was tabulated, Samara handed over the additional cash.

"The train that the rigs need to be on departs the Yining station at 11:00 p.m."

Samara said that he understood and asked when the crated equipment could be picked up.

"They'll be ready by 7:00 p.m. I see you have your own transports outside," the supervisor said, pointing to the window beyond which the two trucks were parked.

"If you can give me directions to the station, we'll take the crates there."

The supervisor drew a crude map to the train station on a sheet of copy paper and handed it to Samara, indicating as he did that the station was less than twenty minutes away.

Samara left the drilling supply company an hour after he entered. He drove around for the next forty-five minutes, followed by the other truck, looking for a suitable location to get rid of the construction materials so that he could extract the weapons from the vehicles. He found that spot after driving down a back road that eventually led to a ragged and distorted gully that was etched in the hard brown earth. The trucks pulled to the side of the dirt path, and Samara used the forklift to off-load the bricks, concrete, and other construction materials from both trucks, leaving them in a heap to the side of the vehicles. Besides the forklift, the only items kept were the foam packing materials and heavy-duty chains that they'd brought from Grozny.

When Samara returned to the company, he was given the necessary paperwork to transport the drilling rigs along with a key to the crate's pick-proof locks and told to have his trucks go to the loading dock at the rear of the building. There he found two large wooden crates, each attached to a block pallet. The nearly square wooden boxes weighed 2,520 pounds, measured just over four feet in length, and had a height and depth of exactly four feet. The nuclear weapons that would replace them were of similar size and weight and therefore wouldn't arouse the curiosity of railway officials, who would expect a crate containing this type of drilling rig to weigh a certain amount.

The warehouse foreman loaded the crates onto the M35s, and Samara and his men departed thirty minutes after they'd arrived, just as night was erasing the last of the spectacular sunset on the horizon. However, by the time the trucks returned to the clearing where the construction materials had been discarded, it was dark—which Samara had anticipated and planned for. Subsequently, in a choreographed chain of actions, as one of the men pointed his vehicle's headlights at the rear of the other M35, two men pulled out the truck's loading ramps while another started the forklift and backed the crate containing the Diamec off the truck. The process was repeated, and once both crates were on the ground, Samara unlocked the wooden boxes. He then directed the placement of two chains over the forklift's arms and under one of the Diamecs, fastening them together with a heavy steel ring. The forklift operator then slowly lifted the heavy drill out of the crate and placed it to the side. The same procedure was followed with the second drill. As this was happening, two of Samara's men removed the wooden covers hiding the nuclear weapons and the bolts securing their cradles to the shock-absorbing platforms below them. By the time they were done, the forklift operator was done with the Diamecs. The forklift operator drove the machine into one of the trucks and, again using the heavy chains, lifted the cradle and the attached weapon, backed it off the vehicle, and lowered it into the first crate. That process was repeated for the second weapon and crate. When both nuclear devices were inside the crates, Samara followed the instructions given to him by Kasym, which—unknown to Samara—ensured that all five men touched the polonium-210. After removing the two notes from his cousin that Kasym had said would be inside the weapons, and verifying that the arming switch was thrown, Samara reattached the faceplates and discarded the butterfly fasteners.

Once the weapons were placed back inside the trucks, Samara brushed away the sugar-like particles that were adhered to the notes he'd extracted and read the verses from the Koran. He passed them to his men, and the verses seemed to reenergize everyone, who repeatedly exclaimed, "Allahu Akbar!"

The process of swapping the drills with the nuclear devices had gone exactly as planned, except that it had taken twice as long as anticipated because everyone exercised an extremely high degree of caution when handling the weapons. Therefore, they arrived at the railway's cargo warehouse, which was located behind the passenger terminal, thirty minutes prior to their train's departure—an hour later than they'd intended. The cargo terminal was in full swing when the trucks backed up to the loading docks and Samara presented the person who approached them with the transport documents that the company had given him.

Nodding his head that everything seemed to be in order, that person, who turned out to be the night foreman, yelled something to the person operating a nearby forklift, and the crates were removed from the trucks. Samara then directed two of his men to park the vehicles at the far end of the train station's cargo lot, where they would hopefully not arouse attention until after the weapons had detonated. He then walked with his other two men to the passenger terminal and purchased five tickets on the 11:00 p.m. train, which had arrived and was now loading and unloading freight and taking on passengers.

Kvachkov and his men arrived in Yining, the only domestic airport in China's northwest border area with Kazakhstan, on a ten-passenger Chinese puddle jumper from Urumqi. The seats were old and lumpy, the plane smelled of aviation fuel, and the flight attendant who had been serving them burnt coffee was old enough to be everyone's grandmother and could barely squeeze down the narrow aisle.

Before boarding the aircraft in Urumqi, Kvachkov had held a meeting with his men and had gone over what Putin had disclosed. The colonel agreed with the Kremlin's intelligence assessment that the weapons would enter China by truck because that would keep the nuclear devices under the control of the handlers for the maximum amount of time and make it easier to smuggle the weapons into a country whose mass transport points of entry were known to have sophisticated detection devices.

The FSB intelligence data that he'd obtained indicated that there were seven border crossings between the two countries. However, not only was Khorgas the closest, but it also was the busiest because it was close to the main highway artery across Kazakhstan. Kvachkov's internet search revealed that the amount of truck traffic crossing into China each day had outstripped the government's ability to inspect the vehicles and process the paperwork in a timely manner. Therefore, inspectors were always being rushed.

"We'll base our operation in Yining," Kvachkov said. "It's the closest Chinese city with an airport to Khorgas."

"And how do we find the vehicle carrying the weapons?" one of Kvachkov's men asked.

"Our esteemed president has indicated that he has the means to locate the bombs. Therefore, we do what we've done dozens of times before as an instrument of our government— we hurry up and wait."

Russia's stealth drone was a brute. The 20,000-pound manta-winged aircraft named the Skat, the Russian word for stingray, was thirty-four feet in length, had a wingspan of nearly thirty-eight feet, and had an operational ceiling of 36,000 feet. Darting along at five hundred miles per hour, it had an operational range of 2,500 miles. However, if the mission called for increasing that distance, the two internal bays could be used to accommodate fuel bladders. The Kremlin had kept the development and operation of this unmanned aerial vehicle, or UAV, secret from the rest of the world and had intended to keep it that way until the drone was obsolete. However, today Vladimir Putin overruled his generals and ordered the Skat to perform an assignment that could bring it and its capabilities to the attention of China and the United States.

Mission control for these aircraft, most of which were disbursed along the borders of the country's sixteen neighboring countries, was at Khotilovo, a secret military airfield north of Moscow. The Skats tasked with spying on northwest China were based two thousand miles away in Novokuznetsk, a desolate area of southwestern Siberia, 731 miles north of Yining.

Senior Lieutenant Grigory Ivashin, who was the primary pilot of a manta-winged aircraft based in Novokuznetsk, was standing near his command console when a technician who'd previously performed preventive maintenance on his console approached and told him that they'd been ordered to install a software update. Since updates were a common occurrence on the Skat, Ivashin stood to the side and watched as the tech inserted a flash drive into the computer port. He was about to ask what the update entailed when he felt a tap on his shoulder. Ivashin turned around.

"Come with me" were the only words the colonel in charge of the Skat program, who was devoid of both personality and empathy, uttered in his monotone voice before leading the way to his glass-enclosed office at the rear of the large rectangular room from which the pilots flew their UAVs.

After Ivashin entered, the colonel told him to close the glass door and have a seat.

"Moscow has given me a highly classified mission that is to be conducted over China."

Ivashin nodded in acknowledgment. Missions over China were common for the Skat.

"This one will be different from past flights in that a special sensor has been installed on your drone. It also won't be a dash-and-return flight because you'll be flying a search pattern in northwest China, looking for whatever it is that this sensor is supposed to detect."

"And if the sensor does find what it's looking for?"

"It'll send a signal to a low-orbiting satellite, which will then relay the signal to this base and to your command console. The software modification that's being installed will set off an indicator light in the lower right-hand corner of your console screen, providing the exact location of whatever the sensor found."

"Whatever that is."

"Your curiosity is an unnecessary distraction. It doesn't matter if the sensor is looking for yak shit or a Chinese missile base. Your responsibility is to fly this grid pattern, period," the colonel said, handing Ivashin a detailed aeronautical map that was broken into grids. "Call me immediately if you get an indicator light. Dismissed."

Ivashin was into the second hour of his grid pattern and bored out of his mind when the red indicator light suddenly started to blink. Zooming in on his navigation console map, he saw that the Skat had just gone over the train station in Yining. Banking the UAV to port and putting it into a circular holding pattern above the station, Ivashin pressed the comm button on his console and touched the number one on the keypad, instantly connecting him to the colonel. Speaking through his headset mic, he informed the colonel and was immediately placed on hold. Twenty seconds later, a man with a crisp baritone voice was conferenced in. Identifying himself as Colonel Vasily Kvachkov, the man took over the conversation and told Ivashin to get high-resolution imagery of the area. The senior lieutenant complied. Cutting the drone's power and bringing it into a tight descending spiral, he quickly descended from 26,000 feet to 5,000 feet. At that altitude the drone's day-night high-resolution cameras could read a newspaper.

"What do you see?" Kvachkov asked.

"A train beside the station, with people getting on and off. Behind the station there appears to be a freight terminal, judging from the loading dock and the two crates on it, one of which is being lifted by a forklift."

"How large are the crates?"

Ivashin told him and then reported that one crate had been taken through what appeared to be a warehouse and loaded onto a freight car.

"Keep that freight car under surveillance. I'll be there in twenty minutes," said Kvachkov.

Flooring the Volvo S60 he'd rented at the Yining airport upon his arrival, Kvachkov got them to the station at 11:10 p.m., ten minutes after the train departed. Telling his men to wait by the car, he ran inside the warehouse, found someone who spoke a little English, and said that he'd been sent to pick up two large crates that were supposed to be waiting for him on the platform. Kvachkov described the crates. The night foreman had a look of confusion on his face as he replied that the paperwork that he'd received clearly indicated that both crates were to be transported by rail to their destination.

Telling Kvachkov to follow, he went to his office, found the crates' transit documents, and showed them to the FSB colonel. However, since they were in Chinese, Kvachkov had no idea what he was looking at. He told the night foreman that he could be holding a recipe for borscht for all he knew.

"Can you at least tell me where these crates are going so that I can stop them along their route?" Kvachkov asked.

"Unless you have written authorization from the sender, that's not going to happen."

"I'll get it."

"Even if you do, the crates have different final destinations," the night foreman said. "Let me write down the routes, and when you get the authorization, you can stop the cargo at one of the stations along the way and have them placed on a train back to Yining."

Kvachkov acknowledged that this was a good idea, and after receiving the train's route, he left the warehouse and called Ivashin, who, as ordered, was keeping his Skat over the train that had departed with the crates.

CHAPTER 13

"**A** LOCAL CAMERA SYSTEM caught the M35s leaving the highway at Yining," Han Li said, returning to the rear of the Z-20 helicopter from the cockpit, where he had just spoken on an encrypted channel with General Chien An, the chief of the general staff of China's People's Liberation Army and a member of Nemesis. "The trucks entered the Yining train station's freight terminal, where each vehicle off-loaded a large square crate."

"That's good news. Are the crates still in the warehouse, or were they put on a train?" Moretti asked, excitement evident in his voice.

"Unfortunately, according to the general, cities the size of Yining aren't given the funds necessary for an extensive urban camera system. Therefore, surveillance cameras at the station monitor only the warehouse loading dock and its adjacent parking lot, to deter cargo theft. The system doesn't record the loading of the freight cars, which occurs on the other side of the warehouse. There's no way to determine if they're still at the station or were placed on the 11:00 p.m. train, which, according to Chien An, was the last to leave Yining. The M35s, interestingly, are still in the parking lot."

"Whoever's in charge at the warehouse could tell us where the crates are."

"Chien An doesn't want to ask anyone at the warehouse about them in case the terrorists are colluding with one or more of the workers. It's better to surprise everyone with our arrival."

Moretti nodded in agreement. "How long till we get to the station?"

"The pilot told me about forty-five minutes. Yan He's aircraft is also diverting there."

"That raises the question of where the terrorists went."

"My guess is that after transporting the weapons across Kazakhstan and smuggling them into China, they're not about to let them out of their sight before they reach their detonation sites. If the devices are in the warehouse, then these men will be close—probably within eyesight of the warehouse. If the bombs were placed on the 11:00 p.m. train, then that's where they'll be."

"Either way, we'd better prepare for a firefight. Anyone willing to kill scores of people with nuclear weapons is likely to fight to the death rather than throw their hands up and surrender. Ever use one of these automatic rifles?" Moretti asked, removing a weapon from a wooden box to his right.

"A few times. It's a QBZ-95-1, a Chinese assault rifle. It's like an AK-74," Han Li said, grabbing one of the weapons from the box and a magazine from a container next to it. "It's standard-issue for anyone in the PLA. Insert the magazine front-first into the well to the rear of the pistol grip, rotate the rear upward into the well until it latches, then pull the charging handle to chamber a round." As she spoke, Han Li demonstrated the instructions she'd given.

Moretti, a former Army Ranger, had fired both an AK-47 and an AK-74 and was familiar with their operation. He quickly installed the remaining magazines and ensured that each assault rifle had a round in its chamber. "We're prepared."

"From our point of view. Unfortunately, it's theirs that counts," Han Li said.

Forty-two minutes later, the two Z-20s landed within seconds of each other in front of the train station's warehouse. In response to the noise, the night foreman and his staff came out of the building to see what was going on. Yan He was the first person off the aircraft and approached the group of men on the platform. With ramrod-straight posture and an unsmiling face, he asked in a gruff voice who was in charge. The night foreman immediately stepped forward and, after a brief conversation, led the lieutenant colonel to his office.

Ten minutes later, Yan He returned and approached the other members of the Nemesis team, who were standing between the helicopters.

"We examined the two M35s at the end of the parking lot," Moretti said. "Their license plates match those that crossed the border at Khorgas. Inside each vehicle, we found that a rear wooden panel concealed a hidden compartment lined with thick slabs of lead."

"That seems to indicate that they were indeed smuggling something radioactive," Yan He replied.

"Are the crates in the warehouse?" Moretti asked.

"Gone. They were loaded yesterday into the freight car on the 11:00 p.m. train. One crate is on its way to Beijing, arriving there at approximately nine thirty tomorrow morning. The other is being transferred in Lanzhou and will get to Shanghai one day later."

"We need to intercept this train while both crates are on it. After that, it's a roll of the dice whether we'll have enough time to retrieve both weapons," Cancelliere said, receiving nods from other members of the team.

"Now that I've given you the good news, let me give you the bad," Yan He said.

The other members of the team looked at him with confusion on their faces, having believed that the separation of the crates in Lanzhou *was* the bad news.

"At eleven ten yesterday evening, someone who spoke English with a Russian accent came to the warehouse and said that he was supposed to pick up these two crates. The foreman, who has worked at this warehouse for ten years and during that time has been approached by more than his fair share of con men, didn't believe the man's story."

"Why?" Bonaquist asked.

"For one thing, each crate had a proper railway shipping document attached to it. Second, a hefty transit fee had been paid to ensure priority delivery of the crates. The foreman felt that it was highly unlikely that anyone who'd pay an express transit fee and go through the trouble of filling out the required forms would confuse how the crates were to be transported, especially since they were being sent to the other end of the country. Third, the person who told this to the foreman arrived at the station in a sedan. If he was there to pick up two crates, where was his truck, since each crate weighed more than a ton?"

"It sounds like the Russians are trying to get their weapons back before they're detonated on Chinese soil," Cancelliere said.

"If the Russians are trying to retrieve these weapons in our homeland without asking for our permission, I believe that President Liu will politically and economically disassociate our country from the Russian Federation," Yan He said.

"If we can get images of the Russians from the warehouse surveillance camera, I'll ask Chien An to circulate their photos to transportation hubs and businesses within a five-hundred-mile radius. They won't be able to refuel their vehicle, eat, change their mode of transport, or sleep anywhere but in their car without being noticed," Han Li said.

"Good thought," Moretti replied. "And what reason do we give if someone asks why they're wanted?"

"We'll think of something. It's one of the advantages of communism," Yan He answered with a smile.

"Getting back to the nuclear weapons," Bonaquist said, looking at Yan He, "how far do you think the train is ahead of us?"

"The foreman estimated it is about 120 miles from the station."

"Does our helicopter have the range to catch it?" asked Moretti, who had taken more than his fair share of special ops helicopter rides.

"I don't know," Yan He replied. He stepped into one of the helicopters and asked the pilot to join their discussion and then presented him with the question.

"The Z-20 has a range of 276 miles at cruise speed, which is slightly under two hundred miles per hour," the pilot answered. "Even with our tanks topped, it's a toss-up whether we can make that round trip without refueling en route since the train will be traveling away from us as we try to intercept it. To complicate matters, we require a specific type of fuel that local airports just don't carry. Yining falls in this category. The nearest military installation where we can obtain that fuel is about thirty minutes northeast of here. I planned to fly there prior to returning to base."

"Can we refuel there and still catch the train?" Bonaquist asked.

"Probably?"

"Then what?" Cancelliere asked. "Politely ask it to stop and hope the terrorists don't have a remote detonator?"

"We rappel from the Z-20 down to it," Bonaquist replied. "We have repelling lines in the aircraft."

"I like that idea, but the Z-20 is extremely noisy," Han Li said. "Everyone on the train will hear us coming, and as Peter said, the terrorists may have a remote detonator."

"Any other ideas?" Moretti asked.

"Just one. But you're not going to like it," Yan He replied.

Kvachkov left the Yining train station with only one destination in mind—the local airport. Time was of the essence, and even if he could forge a document from the sender to return the crates to Yining, there was no guarantee that those who were transporting the weapons would allow that to happen. Therefore, the only plausible course of action, as he had explained to his men, was for them to fly to Lanzhou and take possession of the nuclear devices by bribing the foreman at the rail station with more cash than he'd earn in a lifetime. If that didn't work, they'd quickly and quietly kill the warehouse employees and transport the weapons in whatever truck they could steal to an area where they could be neutralized and hidden.

Using the search engine on his phone, Kvachkov checked the flight schedule and found a flight from Yining to Lanzhou that would get him and his men there long before the train's

4:00 p.m. arrival. Until then, they'd go to the terminal, spread out on the passenger chairs, use the facilities, and be well rested by the time the ticket counter opened. However, as they soon discovered, Yining wasn't Moscow, and when the FSB colonel got to the airport terminal, he found that the doors were locked and the lights were off. A vinyl clock sign affixed to the window adjacent to the front door showed an opening time of 5:00 a.m.

"Yobannye passatizhi!" Kvachkov exclaimed, which literally translated to "fucking pliers" but colloquially meant that this was an unexpected surprise that really pissed him off. "We'll have to go back to the car and try to get some sleep there until the terminal opens."

With no other alternative, they returned to the Volvo. Kvachkov set his watch for 4:50 a.m., leaned back in his seat, and closed his eyes.

It was 3:45 a.m. when the lights on the runway, taxiway, and parking areas of the Yining airport came to life. A Chinese Y-30, a four-engine turboprop that was virtually a duplicate of the American C-130, touched down five minutes later. Six minutes after that, the Z-20s carrying the Nemesis team arrived. Exiting their helicopters, the team ran from the helipad and up the rear loading ramp of the Y-30. Immediately afterward, the turboprop raised its ramp and began to taxi toward the runway. Moments later, it was airborne.

Vasily Kvachkov and his men awoke to a high-pitched whining sound. Looking through the car window and beyond the boundary of the parking lot, they saw that the runway lights were on and that a four-engine Y-30 prop aircraft had landed and was taxiing toward the airport's two helipads, which were on the other side of the boundary fence and two hundred yards directly in front of them. They watched as the cargo aircraft eventually parked perpendicular to the helipads and kept all four engines running at idle as it lowered its loading ramp.

The FSB colonel and his men decided to take a closer look at what was going on and left their vehicle. Walking across the parking lot until they came to the six-foot-high security fence, everyone except for Kvachkov proposed various theories as to why a Chinese Air Force aircraft had set down at the Yining airport at this hour. That question was finally answered six minutes later, when two Chinese military helicopters set down on the helipads. Careful to stay in the unlit shadows, Kvachkov and his men watched as five people, all dressed in US military flight suits, with one or more assault rifles slung over their shoulders, dashed from the helicopters and onto the transport. Kvachkov noted that three of the five appeared to be American. Since he didn't believe in coincidence, he had a sinking feeling in the pit of his stomach that both their missions were aligned.

"We may have competition in retrieving the devices in Lanzhou," Kvachkov said. "The firepower they have on that aircraft effectively neutralizes what we have planned."

"Then what do we do?" asked one of Kvachkov's men.

"Change the field of play."

"I can't even pronounce the name of the town we're flying to," Bonaquist said, following several attempts from Han Li to help him pronounce Daheyanzhen.

"We'll make this easy, Jack," Moretti said. "We'll refer to it as *D*."

"I like that."

"Let me look over everyone one last time before we jump out of this perfectly safe aircraft," Moretti said as he began to check the team's parachutes and helmets, with attached night-vision goggles, all of which the Chinese military had placed on board thanks to a call from President Liu. The ex–Army Ranger, who was an experienced jumper, then repeated the instructions he'd given earlier. Once that was done, they waited for the pilot to tell them when they were over the town.

"What altitude do you want to jump from?" Bonaquist asked.

"Five thousand feet," Yan He answered, having been told earlier by Moretti what altitude to give the pilot.

"That's more than enough," Moretti added. "If something goes wrong with anyone's main chute, there'll be time to activate the reserve. Remember, the static line from your chute connects to this cable," he said, touching the cable above his head. "When you jump, it'll automatically deploy the chute. If something goes wrong, which means your chute doesn't open when you leave the aircraft, just pull your reserve handle." Moretti pointed to it.

"Is there some reason we can't find an airport near D and take a vehicle there?" Bonaquist asked.

"Time is of the essence. The faster we secure the weapons, the less of a chance the Russians will get to them before us, which is why we're parachuting."

"Two minutes," the pilot announced over the speaker.

"Everyone stand and connect to the cable," Moretti said, beginning his check of everyone's static line connection. When he was done, he gave a thumbs-up sign to the crew chief.

The aircraft's cargo door opened.

"Thirty seconds," the pilot said.

Bonaquist, who was the closest to the door, felt a firm shove from behind and was launched out of the aircraft as the pilot yelled "go."

Han Li, the instigator of Bonaquist's sudden departure, was the next to go, and Moretti was the last.

Kvachkov and his men entered the airport at 5:00 a.m., went straight to the China Southern ticket counter, purchased their tickets, and then passed through security. Kvachkov then sent his team to get something to eat while he proceeded to the departure gate. As he was walking, he called Ivashin, who reported that the Skat was still following the train from Yining and could stay over it as far as Lanzhou before it had to return to its base in the southwestern Siberian city of Novokuznetsk to refuel.

"I need you to be on the alert for a Chinese aircraft that resembles the American C-130," Kvachkov cautioned, getting straight to the point of his call without any preamble or semblance of cordiality. "I believe those aboard this aircraft will either try to parachute onto the train or block the tracks so that it must stop. Therefore, I suggest you place your drone at an altitude where their aircraft won't detect you. Call me at the first sign of conflict." Kvachkov then ended the call without further explanation.

As he was nearing his gate, he noticed an airport security officer holding a photo in his right hand and comparing the faces of those in the waiting area to it. Curious, Kvachkov casually approached the officer from behind and, being six inches taller than the officer, looked over his shoulder. Stunned, he saw that the man was holding a photograph of him. Kvachkov did an immediate about-face and quickly walked away. As he did, he saw his men walking toward him.

"The restaurant is closed," said one of his men as they converged.

"Forget about the food. The security officer behind me has my photograph and is obviously looking for me. I'm not sure if he knows what flight I'm on or is searching the entire terminal."

"How?" another team member asked.

"The how isn't important. This terminal is small, and sooner or later, he'll spot me."

"Boarding starts in fifteen minutes," one of his men said. "Perhaps we can get on the plane before he sees us."

"He's probably going to be watching our gate because our flight is the next to board. Therefore, we must unobtrusively kill him before then. It goes without saying that if his death is noticed before our departure, then the police will seal the terminal and prevent any flights from departing."

The plan they devised on the fly was simple, and Kvachkov initiated it by walking briskly past the officer and brushing his shoulder to get his attention. He continued his casual pace and entered a restroom, which Kvachkov's men had partially blocked off by rolling an unattended janitorial cart in front of it. As soon as the officer followed him inside, one of Kvachkov's men put him in a choke hold. Thirty seconds later, the asphyxiated officer was dragged into the farthest stall and set on the toilet, and the door was latched. One of the men removed the cart from the door, and Kvachkov and his men proceeded to their gate.

CHAPTER 14

THE SENIOR SENATOR from Illinois was impressed with the latest photos he had received from Beck, each of which had an intelligence narrative on the back. The first picture showed two Chinese helicopters, described as Z-20s, landing at a train station in Yining, a city the DOD indicated had no known military significance. The next showed these aircraft on helipads at the local airport. The five passengers aboard, who previous surveillance had shown at the Chinese air base in northwest China, were shown in the next photo to be walking up the ramp of a Y-30 Chinese military aircraft. Each person carried one or more assault weapons slung over their shoulder and a sidearm on their hip.

"This isn't a cooperative summit," Lynn said to himself. "This is a joint covert op."

Lynn continued looking at the photos. The next one was an infrared image of five people, their faces obscured by helmets, jumping from the Y-30. The one after that showed five parachutes descending toward a train station in a town whose name he couldn't pronounce. The last infrared photo was of a Russian Skat, a drone previously brought to the attention of the DOD by a defector and so highly classified within the Russian Federation that there was no official acknowledgment that it even existed, flying above a train headed toward the town with the difficult name. The fact that a super-secret Russian drone was this far into China meant that whatever the Russians were up to, it had to be extraordinarily important for them to risk the discovery or loss of such an asset.

"Let me sort through this," Lynn muttered to himself. "Two Asians visit Site R, then join three Americans at Joint Base Andrews, where they're placed into the back seats of five F-16s. Apparently, time is of the essence since they refuel in the air, racing halfway across the world to an aging Sino air base. Once they land, there's no welcome event. Instead they're issued tactical gear, placed in two Chinese military helicopters, and flown to a train station in a town known for mining and fruit production. They remain at the station for only a matter of minutes before taking off, this time for a pinprick of a town that's unpronounceable by Westerners and that US intelligence says has no strategic importance. Nevertheless, these five people execute a nighttime low-level parachute jump onto the grounds of the town's train station. To confuse things even more, a Russian drone, so classified that neither the Russians nor our DOD publicly acknowledges its existence, is following a train headed toward this station. What the hell are Ballinger, Putin, and President Liu after on that train that's apparently time-sensitive and critical to each nation?"

Lynn grabbed a bottle of brown water, poured four fingers of the eighty-six-proof scotch into a crown-cut double old-fashioned glass, and reclined in his La-Z-Boy as he tried to connect the dots and answer his own question. Twenty minutes later, with not an inkling of what was in the pot of the high-stakes poker game being played by three countries,

Lynn decided that it was time to ratchet things up a little so that he could find out.

In a country with 1.4 billion people, the 50,000 residents of Daheyanzhen were a micro-miniscule part of China's population. The town's main source of revenue was the manufacture of cheap parts for Urumqi. Because of its lower labor and operating costs, it was able to produce these parts 30 percent cheaper than they could be manufactured in larger Chinese cities. This manufacturing efficiency had a dark side, however—the workers' salaries were necessarily low, and workplace conditions were less than desirable to maintain this manufacturing advantage. Therefore, although business owners raked in the cash, it was difficult for them to expand or even maintain their workforce, because no one who had a choice wanted to work for low wages in a town that essentially was surrounded by a barren wasteland.

Daheyanzhen's main thoroughfare was Yanguan Street, off which ran half a dozen avenues. South of this small cluster of commercialization was the railway station, which was the town's lifeline, receiving raw materials and delivering its finished products.

The five members of the Nemesis team landed, some softer than others, on the grassy field behind the railway station. If the 11:00 p.m. train from Yining kept to its schedule, it would arrive at first light, which was ten minutes away. Yan He reached into his pants pocket, grabbed a pair of insignias bearing two gold stars between two parallel gold lines—the PLA rank of lieutenant colonel—and pinned one on each shoulder of his tactical uniform. He then led the team into the station's freight office. Yan He approached the nineteen-year-old employee inside and told him that he and his team would be appropriating two crates, which he would point out, from the arriving train's freight car. The employee, not about to argue with a PLA officer, led the team onto the platform, where he started an aging forklift and moved it into position to unload not only the crates mentioned by the PLA officer but also the raw materials for the town's factories.

The train arrived exactly on schedule, and once it came to a stop, the employee threw open the door to the freight car. Yan He, Cancelliere, and Bonaquist then stepped in front of the employee and immediately entered. At the same time this was happening, Moretti and Han Li began walking through the passenger cars, looking for the five men who had crossed the border at Khorgas, whose photos had been sent to their cell phones.

Fifteen minutes after the search began, it was over. The five men and the crates from Yining had disappeared.

Jabir Samara had dark circles under his eyes, vision that was beginning to blur, and an encroaching lethargy that was draining energy from his body. He attributed these maladies to a combination of stress and a bug that he'd somehow caught in this unholy part of the world. Even so, his mission was proceeding smoothly. Removing the crates at the train stop in Urumqi had taken some doing. He'd first had to convey what he wanted to the station's freight coordinator, who spoke only rudimentary English. Time and again, the man had indicated that Samara's request was impossible to grant. The railroad had strict rules on the handling and delivery of its cargo, and these must be obeyed. It was the law. However, as with most situations in China, the right amount of cash could alter a person's perception of what was possible, and after Samara handed the man the equivalent of five years' pay, the coordinator had directed the warehouse employees who worked for him to off-load the two crates from the Yining train.

Once the train had departed for Daheyanzhen, the next stop on its journey toward Lanzhou, the freight coordinator pocketed an additional year's salary by filling out new transit documents and agreeing to use the station's trucks to deliver the weapons to the Urumqi airport's freight terminal, which was only seven and a half miles away. The cost to transport over two tons by air was an astronomical number but would be ignored by those at the airport because Samara had paid this fee at the train station and acquired the necessary chops and stamps on the transit documents to certify that inspection and payment had been done.

Once the crates were loaded onto the trucks, Samara and his men got into the vehicles and accompanied the drivers to the Urumqi airport's freight terminal. Since the paperwork had been completed, the transit fees had been paid, and the aircraft they were going on were sitting on the tarmac, both crates were immediately processed for loading. Each was weighed, transferred to a scissor-lift vehicle, and driven to its respective aircraft—one going to Beijing and the other to Shanghai.

The Russian embassy was situated on Mount Alto, the third-largest hill in Washington, DC. Formerly the site of a Veterans Administration hospital, it commanded a magnificent view of the White House, Pentagon, and State Department. It was also a source of irritation and concern to the intelligence community, who feared that this line of sight gave the Russians an advantage in electronically spying on some of the most sensitive buildings in Washington.

The vice chairman of the Senate Select Committee on Intelligence arrived at the embassy's weekly cultural affairs party an hour after its official start time. Everyone in attendance knew that these functions, which brought the elite of many governments into the embassy, had nothing to do with acquiring a better understanding of a country's culture. Instead, they were about intelligence gathering—for both the Russians and their invitees. Guests on each side hoped that the alcohol, food, and convivial atmosphere could loosen tongues and provide them with valuable information and insights. Since knowledge was the basis of power for those within government and the recognized currency for bartering, the more secrets a person was able to ferret out, the more leverage that person had to obtain what he or she was after. Today, Lynn intended to expend some of that currency to, politically speaking, transform Ballinger from the president into the walking dead.

Lynn knew his way around the embassy. A regular at the weekly functions because of the Balvenie 1972 Vintage Cask scotch that was kept for him under the counter—a scotch that went for over $3,000 a bottle—he always made straight for the bar. He'd figured out quite some time ago that this accommodation had nothing to do with Russian hospitality. It had everything to do with the hope that the rare velvety liquid would cause him to overindulge and loosen his tongue, after which he'd inadvertently reveal information from his committee or his discussions with various intelligence agencies.

The ballroom was near the center of the embassy, which one reached by crossing the lobby and continuing down a long central corridor with white marble floors. The corridor's walls featured portraits of previous Soviet and

Russian ambassadors to the United States, hung against a red background. The good senator from Illinois entered the ballroom and went straight to the bar, which was to the right.

The bartender, an FSB agent who'd memorized the movers and shakers in Washington from a series of flashcards given to him during training, recognized the senator. He reached under the counter, grabbed the bottle of Balvenie, and had poured three fingers of the pale brown liquid into a heavy crystal glass by the time Lynn reached him. The senator finished the glass in three gulps, then asked for a refill. After the bartender complied, Lynn began to mingle, draining his glass twice more in the next hour. Downing twelve fingers of scotch in an hour would make the average person comatose. But as a full-fledged alcoholic, Lynn was only slightly buzzed. On his way back to the bar for round five, he was intercepted by Major Yevgeny Gorkin of the Russian army, who was the embassy's chief political officer as well as the senior FSB official in the United States.

"It's good to see you," Gorkin said, extending his hand.

"I was hoping I'd find you," the senator replied, shaking hands with the five-foot-nine former wrestler, who had exceptionally broad shoulders and a crushing grip.

"And why is that?"

"Because I wanted to congratulate you on the success of your Skat drone program. From what I've heard, even the Chinese can't detect it."

Gorkin gently guided Lynn to a spot away from anyone who might be listening. "Thank you for your vote of confidence in our technology, but the program to which you're referring was canceled years ago. It never got past the prototype stage. It was abandoned because we're working hard on the next-generation drone."

"Yeah, I heard about that. Nuclear-powered, right? I also heard that the engineers working on this drone were easy to spot because they glowed in the dark. Come off it, Eugene," Lynn said, addressing the major by the nickname used by those who had a working relationship with him. "The only way you're going to solve the power problem for that drone is to get better hackers to penetrate Boeing's computer system, which I'm told you attempt numerous times a day."

"I'll pass those comments to Moscow, along with your government's inaccurate belief that they detected a Skat over China."

"Eugene, don't bullshit a bullshitter. I can send you a photo of the Skat, which is over China at this very moment. In fact, why don't I give a copy of that picture to the Chinese ambassador? I believe I see him at the other end of the room. Perhaps he can send a couple of fighters up to photograph it before they put it into the ground and steal your technology. That assumes, of course, that they don't want to make this intrusion an international incident."

The expression on Gorkin's face changed from placidity to one of confusion. Lynn, who was good at reading people, noticed that Gorkin raised his left eyebrow and pursed his lips together, a dead giveaway that the major was surprised to hear what he'd been told.

"Why don't I refill that drink?" Gorkin replied as he guided Lynn back to the bar and asked the bartender to hand him the bottle of Balvenie. "Maybe we should continue this conversation in the Fireplace Hall. It's a comfortable room, and we can get away from those who might want to hear what we're discussing."

Lynn agreed, and Gorkin led him past a set of plainclothes guards at the far end of the ballroom and down a hallway whose walls were lined with photographs of past Soviet and Russian presidents. Eventually, they entered a room dominated by a large fireplace.

"Please have a seat," Gorkin said, pointing with an outstretched arm to a black tufted leather club chair beside the fireplace. He then refilled the senator's glass and sat in an adjoining chair.

Lynn took a long swig of scotch, then set his glass down on a side table.

"What you probably saw was Boeing's Phantom Ray drone, which looks remarkably like our Skat, which, as I said, is not operational."

"It should look like Boeing's drone since you stole their engineering plans. That aside, an American aircraft wouldn't have the Russian Federation flag painted on its fuselage."

"Let me verify what you've told me with Moscow, as sometimes I'm kept in the dark. If I've been left out of this loop, then perhaps I could use your help to avert a particularly nasty diplomatic situation. In return, I'm sure there's something I can do for you."

"Let's meet tomorrow at the Capital Grille on Pennsylvania Avenue at 2:00 p.m. I'll be sitting at a table in the back."

"I look forward to it."

Gorkin arrived at the Capital Grille fifteen minutes ahead of his scheduled meeting with Rufus Lynn and found the Illinois senator at his customary table with an empty drink glass in front of him. Once he was seated, a waiter came forward and asked if they'd like a drink. Lynn pointed to his glass, indicating that he wanted a refill, while Gorkin ordered water. Once the waiter had left, Lynn took several photos from his jacket pocket, laid them facedown on the table, and slid the top one across the crisp white tablecloth. Gorkin examined it closely before sliding it back.

"As you can see, that's a photograph of an operational Skat. It's not nice to lie to someone who's trying to help you, Eugene."

Gorkin was about to respond when the waiter returned with their drinks, after which Lynn sent him away, saying they'd order food later.

"I apologize. It's a force of habit due to my occupation," Gorkin said once they were alone.

"As my dear mother used to say, it is what it is."

"Who else has seen these?"

"As far as I know, only my contact at the DOD. However, I'm sure he's blabbed to his boss and this photo is working its way up their chain of command."

"Can you sweep this matter under the carpet, so to speak?" Gorkin asked, taking a sip of water.

"Possibly. If I do, I'll need an equally difficult favor."

Gorkin nodded, seeming to understand that barters worked only if the things they were negotiating had similar values. "Understood. What do you require for this favor?"

Lynn put a photo in front of Gorkin. "This is a group of Chinese and American individuals who were at the train station in Yining. The train your UAV is following left that station last night, Chinese time. I want to know what's on that train. Your government would not be using its most sophisticated drone to follow an ancient piece of locative equipment from a no-name town, and my country wouldn't be sending people halfway around the world to the train station it left, unless there was something extremely important to both countries on board. I want to know what that is."

"I don't have access to every intelligence operation my government conducts. If the Kremlin sent a drone into China, very few people would know about it."

"I don't want excuses, only the answer to my question, Eugene. If you don't want to tell me, perhaps you can inform President Liu when he summons your ambassador to his office."

"I'll try, but it will take time," Gorkin replied, his voice losing its formerly confident tone.

"Let me help speed things up. Tell Putin that he has until this time tomorrow to respond, or he's going to have one pissed-off neighbor accusing him in front of the world of being unneighborly. It'll be a PR nightmare. Oh, and just in case you're thinking I may be in ill health and could die at any moment, remember that the DOD has these photos. However, because of my position in Congress, my vote and the recommendations of my committee are more valuable to the DOD than exposing your misdeed."

"Now that each of us has set our expectation, I'll see you here at the same time tomorrow," Gorkin said, hastily getting up from the table.

Lynn summoned the waiter, ordered a glass of twenty-five-year-old Macallan's scotch, and downed the smooth liquid as if drinking water on a hot day. Since his committee meeting didn't start for an hour, he held up the now empty glass before the waiter could even leave the table, indicating that he wanted another.

CHAPTER 15

K VACHKOV WAS A skeptic who didn't believe in coincidence, especially in a town the size of Yining, and he was certain that everyone lied to advance their agenda. Everyone. These opinions were in line with his training and years of service at the FSB. Consequently, he had been able to accept only one explanation for the Chinese military aircraft being in Yining at the hour he spotted it: it was there to pick up a team to intercept the train he was after and retrieve the nuclear weapons. Assuming that was true, his own interdiction had to occur prior to the crates reaching Lanzhou. Since Kvachkov knew he'd be outgunned in any type of conflict he might have with this team, he had concluded that he needed a change in plan, which was why he'd flown from Yining to Urumqi instead of Lanzhou. Since this was the first stop the train would make after leaving Yining, there was a good chance he'd get to the crates first.

He called Ivashin immediately after exiting the aircraft, wanting to know the exact location of the train and how far it was from Urumqi. That's when he received two pieces of information that put a large ragged hole in his assumption that he'd get to the crates first: the train was now beyond Urumqi, and the Skat no longer registered the signature of deflecting muons. Fortunately, Kvachkov was left in his abyss of despair for only seconds before Ivashin informed him that he had reversed the drone and started a widening circle pattern and eventually had found the deflecting muon signature at the Urumqi airport's cargo terminal.

Kvachkov, who'd just disembarked his aircraft seconds ago, was in the Urumqi passenger terminal. He looked out the floor-to-ceiling windows he was standing near and stared at three hangars clustered together three hundred yards away. There he spotted two large scissor-lift vehicles, each transporting a large crate. Watching the vehicles as they crossed the tarmac, he saw that each loaded its cargo onto a different commercial aircraft. There was no doubt in his mind what was in each crate.

Ten yards to the right of Kvachkov and his team, Samara and his men looked out the Urumqi airport's floor-to-ceiling windows and watched their weapons of mass destruction being loaded. The aircraft carrying the nuclear device to Beijing took off thirty minutes later, and the one to Shanghai departed fifteen minutes after that. Their job was done. Samara was happy that he and his men would return home as heroes, and he assured his men that stories of what they'd done today would be retold by the faithful for generations.

Their flight to Astana, Kazakhstan, would take them in the opposite direction of the nuclear weapons' destination. That was by design because the electromagnetic pulse, or EMP, that resulted from the nuclear explosions would destroy the electronics of anything it impacted, on the ground or in the air. That meant that every aircraft in its blast radius would fall from the sky. Once they reached Astana, he and his men would fly to Dubai, and from there they would travel to Islamabad, Pakistan.

Samara was one of the last to board, and as he walked to the rear of the aircraft, he could see his men scattered throughout the economy-class cabin. All had their eyes closed and seemed to be trying to get some much-needed rest. Five minutes after he took his seat, the cabin door closed, and the Airbus A330 backed away from the gate. Twenty minutes later, it was airborne. Samara felt nauseous and had a headache. The good news, as far as he was concerned, was that he was next to a restroom. With no one in the two seats next to him, he lay across all three and fastened a seat belt around his body. He had just dozed off when he was awoken by a chorus of voices around him.

"Don't touch him," a female flight attendant was saying as Samara sat up.

Samara looked down the aisle and saw that one of his men was lying five feet from him with his eyes wide open, blood coming from the corners of his mouth. Seconds later, a woman several rows in front of him stood and screamed as she pointed to the lifeless man next to her. Samara tuned out the next scream. He knew that another of his men was dying or dead and that soon they all would be dead. With an expression of resignation on his face, he placed a pillow behind his neck and reclined his seat to the limit, which was just two inches. He instantly understood that their deaths and his were from being exposed to a lethal amount of radiation; Samara just wasn't sure whether this had happened by accident or had been arranged by his cousin. Either way, the result was the same.

When Gorkin arrived for his meeting with Lynn, the senator had an empty glass in front of him, and the waiter was setting down its replacement. As with their first meeting, Gorkin asked for a glass of water.

After the waiter brought the water and left again, Gorkin moved his glass to the side, removed a photo from his jacket pocket, and handed the photo to Lynn. "I believe this is what you're looking for."

Lynn's eyes went wide when he saw a photo of two large bombs.

"Are these what I think they are?"

Gorkin simply nodded. "I'm fairly certain that your president and one or more of your security agencies know at least part of what I'm about to tell you," Gorkin said, seemingly enjoying, from the grin on his face, the fact that he'd surprised Lynn. "What you're looking at is a Soviet-era nuclear weapon weighing slightly more than one ton. During the Cold War we sent these to satellite countries to better disperse our nuclear arsenal. In all, five hundred of these nuclear devices were manufactured. Unfortunately, only 498 were accounted for in the end. The two missing weapons had been stored at a military base in Grozny."

"Chechnya," Lynn said in a derogatory tone.

"A thorn in my government's side, to be sure. Timing is everything, and the theft happened the day the Soviet Union broke up into the Russian Federation and a number of independent countries. Moscow was in a state of chaos, and our record-keeping and security protocols were a mess. Therefore, it took time to discover that these weapons were missing. Our investigation concluded that the base commander, Major General Vitaly Barinov, sold the nuclear devices to an unknown party, although we never discovered the bank account to which that money was sent. Notwithstanding, Barinov issued passes and the necessary paperwork to allow two milling machines to leave the base hours before Russian military aircraft were to transport all nuclear devices to Moscow. He also did several other things, which I won't disclose, that allowed the weapons to leave the secure bunkers in which they were stored."

"Where is General Barinov now?"

"Dead. His body was found the morning the weapons were to be transported back to Moscow."

"What are you telling me, Eugene?"

"That we're trying to retrieve these weapons in China and that the Skat you photographed is tracking them by means of a sophisticated sensor it has on board. However, we're not the only country looking for these devices. The US and Chinese governments are also trying to retrieve them."

"Who's behind smuggling them into the country, and why the hell do they want to blow up China? The United States is everyone's favorite target."

"The answer to your first question is Awalmir Afridi."

"He's dead."

Gorkin shook his head in the negative. "The answer to your second question is that Afridi probably didn't believe he could smuggle the weapons into the United States, but he could get them into China—which he obviously has."

"This is interesting, Eugene, but I need dirt on President Ballinger. Working with the Chinese in secret to prevent a nuclear holocaust in China's homeland would be considered noble not only by most Americans but also by the world community. However, I have a question. Obviously, your government never informed the Chinese about the nuclear devices or the fact that your drone was tracking them.

Although I understand why you didn't want to tell the Chinese that you violated their airspace, why not tell them about the weapons?"

"These nuclear weapons must never be traced back to Moscow. If they're detonated, China would hold us accountable. If they're retrieved by the US and Chinese forces, then it brings up the question of what other Soviet or Russian devices are missing and kept secret. No amount of reassurance on our part would ever put that issue to rest and restore confidence in our nuclear security procedures. However, if we retrieve these devices, then this situation never happened."

"It should be quite a meet-and-greet if your force gets to the weapons at the same time as the Chinese and the Americans. What is Putin going to tell President Liu when he asks why he's conducting a covert operation on Chinese soil?"

Gorkin didn't answer. Instead, he implied what he wanted from their meeting. "If the weapons are detonated or captured by the Chinese and Americans, you're in an excellent position to control the narrative. As the vice chairman of the Senate Select Committee on Intelligence, you can let it be known that these nuclear devices came from another country, such as Pakistan. We sold them nuclear devices during the Cold War."

"And denied that to us."

"Nevertheless."

"If I do make this statement, where's my proof?"

"I'll provide that to you if the time comes."

"Do you think I'm that naive? My head's on the chopping block, not yours."

Gorkin paused for a full thirty seconds as he deliberated what he was about to say. "I'll provide internal Soviet records verifying the sale of these weapons to Pakistan, providing the serial numbers of the missing weapons as proof. You can come up with a story about the anonymous source that provided them to you."

"Your government will take a lot of heat, especially from Pakistan. They'll know you set them up."

"Their government and intelligence services protect terrorists. No one will believe their denials. In any event, my country has little choice given the circumstances."

"Now that we've discussed how to save your bacon, what's in it for me, Eugene?"

"This," Gorkin said, removing several pieces of paper from his jacket pocket and handing them to Lynn.

The senator read what he'd been given, then turned the papers facedown on the table. "Is this real?" Lynn asked, his face going flush as increased adrenaline caused dilation of blood vessels and a rapid increase in heart rate.

"The conversation you just read, between Lieutenant Colonel Cray, formerly of the US Army Intelligence and Security Command, and former Special Agent Jack Bonaquist, was recorded by one of our agents on the National Mall. Apparently, they meet frequently at this spot because it's easy to see if they've been followed or are being spied on. However, the person aiming a laser listening device at them from a bench five hundred yards away goes unnoticed. As you read, both are now part of an off-the-book military team known as Nemesis, which seems to be under the control of President Ballinger and President Liu of China. Its purpose, from what we've pieced together from these conversations, appears to be to conduct covert operations without the oversight of either government. Essentially, both presidents have set up an unaccountable private army with headquarters at your Raven Rock Mountain Complex."

Lynn seemed to slip deep in thought, where he remained for about ten seconds before coming out of his trance. "I'll need the recordings."

"I'll have them delivered to your office by private courier. The sender will be a prominent DC law firm. Do we have a deal?"

"We do."

"Then congratulations, Mr. President."

Vladimir Putin couldn't sleep. That should have been unusual for someone who had ironclad control over his country's political system and ruthlessly eliminated his rivals so that he seldom had to watch his back. The reason for his insomnia was China. If the two nuclear bombs that Kvachkov was chasing detonated there, the origin of these weapons would be known with absolute certainty. He couldn't blame China for the nuclear mishap. Nor could he blame a rogue country, such as North Korea or Iran, for smuggling the weapons into China and setting them off. The head of his country's nuclear program had explained to him, when he asked how anyone could prove the origin of a nuclear weapon since it would be vaporized in the explosion, that each nuclear explosion left unique fingerprints of sorts. The most common of these was the ratio of the isotopes the weapon contained and the composition of the bomb's tamper, the spherical shell that kept the core from flying apart too quickly. Each nation manufacturing nuclear weapons, as it turned out, had its own recipe. Therefore, once the weapon's origin was determined from the debris, such as melted sand, the world would know that the Russian Federation was indirectly responsible for what had occurred. China would angrily accuse Russia of negligence for failing to secure its nuclear stockpile. The resulting rift between the countries would be economically catastrophic for the Russian Federation since the Chinese had recently signed a $400 billion thirty-year contract to purchase their natural gas, on top of a ten-year $85 billion contract to buy oil. If they canceled these contracts, the Russian Federation would become insolvent and economically implode in much the same manner as the former Soviet Union.

Currently, the only life preserver that Putin had to get him out of this mess, should Kvachkov fail, was made of recycled paper. The plan relied on an alcoholic US senator from Illinois who, according to Gorkin, was amenable to pinning the mishap on Pakistan, a past purchaser of nuclear devices from the Soviet Union. In return, the senator was getting recordings implicating Ballinger in a host of illegal activities. However, the attempt to blame Pakistan would be exposed as bullshit if the Chinese discovered Kvachkov and his men on their soil using a Russian drone to help them chase the train on which the weapons were transported. Therefore, the colonel and his team needed to leave China as quickly as possible. The fact that the Chinese had Kvachkov's photo and were currently looking for him could easily be blamed on a facial recognition software error or other reason his technical people had yet to give him. Once Kvachkov crossed the border into Russia, he'd be given an impenetrable alibi and scores of witnesses who could attest that he had never left Moscow.

CHAPTER 16

S TANDING ON THE train platform in the town whose name no one could pronounce, the Nemesis team didn't need a rocket scientist in their ranks to figure out that the crates had been removed in Urumqi since that was the only stop the Yining train had made before this. Once that was determined, Yan He called Chien An. After that, things happened quickly. The chief of the general staff of the People's Liberation Army called the Urumqi train station's now wealthy freight coordinator and found out that two large crates had been off-loaded from the 11:10 p.m. Yining train at his station and taken to the cargo terminal at the airport. The coordinator never considered lying to the most powerful military person in the country. He knew that if he did, he'd never get an opportunity to spend the money he'd received.

Chien An's next call was to the Urumqi airport's freight terminal. He discovered that the two crates delivered from the train station had been loaded onto separate commercial aircraft, a China Airlines flight going to Beijing and a China Southern aircraft flying to Shanghai. Both had already taken off.

Most considered the head of China's military to be the most powerful person in the country since he ensured that the

165

Communist Party, and consequently the current government, remained in power. He also oversaw the country's black prisons, which, although not publicly acknowledged, were known by everyone to exist. Therefore, when he called the air traffic control supervisor to have the Air China and China Southern flights return to Urumqi, explaining that there was a military exercise in the area and the airspace was now restricted, no questions were asked.

Within an hour, both aircraft landed in Urumqi, and their highly irate passengers deplaned. As that occurred, the freight coordinator supervised the removal of the crates from the aircraft and their transport to a hangar, where he placed them under heavy guard until the Nemesis team arrived.

The Y-30 landed in Daheyanzhen on an uneven strip of dirt, not much wider than the width of its main landing gear, and came to a stop close to where the Nemesis team stood. Once airborne, the pilot put the pedal to the metal. At this speed, it would take a little less than twenty minutes to cover the 115 miles from Daheyanzhen to the Urumqi airport and taxi to the hangar containing the nuclear weapons.

During the flight Moretti and Han Li decided to do a back-of-the-envelope calculation as to when the bombs might detonate, believing that the terrorists would have ensured that the weapons would explode even if they were killed. They agreed that there was no downside to making that assumption. Before doing their calculation, they went to the cockpit and asked the copilot some questions, while the pilot remained focused on getting the aircraft to its destination as quickly as possible. In response, the copilot told them that it took a commercial jet approximately three and a half hours to fly from Urumqi to Beijing and half an hour longer from

Urumqi to Shanghai, with descent beginning thirty minutes prior to landing in each case. Returning to the rear of the aircraft, Moretti and Han Li discussed what they knew.

"Five terrorists drove these weapons through Kazakhstan and into northwest China. At that time the weapons wouldn't have been armed because delays due to weather, issues with roads, vehicle malfunctions, getting lost, and so forth would have been unforeseen possibilities over which they had no control."

Han Li concurred.

"They took the weapons, which were hidden in crates, and dropped them off at the Yining train station for transport to Beijing and Shanghai, which are probably their intended targets."

"We have to assume that the detonation timer in each weapon was set by that time," Han Li continued. "Since the trains in my country rarely deviate from schedule, the timers could have been set to ignite the devices in the center of those cities, since that's where the main train stations are located."

"But whether by design or through a change in plans— we'll never know—they removed the crates in Urumqi and put them aboard commercial aircraft. The destinations are the same, but the time of detonation would be advanced now," Moretti said.

"Therefore, these weapons must contain a second timer, one that's activated when the bombs pass through a certain altitude."

"Circuitry that allows for the airborne arming of ordnance has been around since before I was in the military. If you think about it, setting a timer before the weapons were loaded on the aircraft would be dicey since commercial flights can be delayed because of weather, mechanical problems, a sick passenger, and so on. However, there's also the possibility that one of the terrorists has a handheld trigger."

"I thought about that," Han Li said, "but it's questionable whether this device would be able to send a signal that would penetrate the contents of the cargo hold to ignite the weapon. Metal parts or steel containers in the body of the aircraft might deflect the signal. After all, the terrorists wouldn't know the contents of the cargo hold. As carefully as this operation seems to have been planned, especially after all it took to transport these weapons into China, I don't believe they'd take a chance on a handheld trigger. That's assuming the trigger wasn't confiscated at security because no one knew what the heck it was."

"Therefore, an altitude-activated timer seems to make sense," Moretti said.

"Again, since we don't have a downside in making that assumption, let's go with it."

After coming to the conclusion that the terrorists likely would have adjusted the altitude activation settings so that both bombs would explode simultaneously, while one aircraft was on approach and the other just beginning to make its descent, they believed they would have only an hour to an hour and a half after they landed in Urumqi to disarm both weapons.

"Ever disarm a bomb?"

Han Li shook her head in the negative. "I don't believe that's something we can Google. But I know someone who can get us the help we need." Returning to the cockpit, she called General Chien An from the copilot's communications console and requested a nuclear weapons expert to talk them through the disarming process.

The Y-30 taxied off the runway and was guided by the tower to a group of three hangars, coming to a stop in front of the one with heavy security in front of it. Apparently, the guards had been told to expect them and now opened the hangar door for the five team members and allowed them access. It didn't hurt that Yan He was wearing the rank of lieutenant colonel. The soldiers stood at attention and saluted as he walked past them.

The team went straight to the crates. Seeing that they were locked, Moretti found a bolt cutter on a nearby bench, sheared the locks off, and gently opened each crate's lid. Inside each was a Soviet-era nuclear weapon.

"Let's get the general's expert on the phone," Moretti said.

Han Li called Chien An, who conferenced in a nuclear weapons expert from Beijing. Han Li then handed the phone to Moretti. Thankfully, the expert spoke English. Otherwise, Han Li would have needed to interpret.

The nuclear weapons expert asked Moretti to describe the weapons in detail and to give the numbers, if any, that were painted on the side of them. Moretti read off the numbers.

A minute later, presumably after consulting reference material or a database, the expert said, "These are nuclear devices."

"Do they have a timer?"

"Each weapon has two—one for a ground detonation and one for an airborne blast. That provided the Soviets with the mission flexibility to attack almost any target." He then asked Moretti to remove the faceplates, in order to cut the wires necessary to disarm the weapons.

"That's going to be a problem," Moretti said, "because the screws, if that's what you call them, have no cuts on top. They're smooth. There's a space surrounding them where it looks like some sort of tool latches on to their serrated edges and allows them to be turned."

"I was afraid of that. You'll need a very specific butterfly fastener to remove them. Fasteners of this type were commonly used in weapons from this era to facilitate maintenance and arming," the expert said. "They were then removed prior to transport to prevent tampering. This complicates things significantly."

"How significantly?"

"Without the fasteners, you need to drill out the screws. Given the hardness of the bomb casing, that's going to be extremely time-consuming."

"Will it take longer than an hour?"

"Significantly longer," the expert replied. "That doesn't include the time it'll take me to talk you through the disarming process."

"If these nuclear devices are set to explode within the next ninety minutes, then there's no possible way to prevent detonation."

"None."

The plan, which was more an idea than a detailed outline of actions, came from Han Li and was immediately green-lighted by President Liu. It came about when she walked outside the hangar to get some fresh air and looked at the barren landscape surrounding the airport. It was then that she recalled a tragedy that had occurred in 2014, not far from where she was standing. Sixteen men had been working in an underground Urumqi coal mine when the tunnel they were in collapsed. Complicating the situation was their inadvertent penetration of an underground stream, which resulted in the mine filling with water, drowning all sixteen men. The accident had received national attention and sparked coal mine reforms throughout the country. This had resulted in the closure of two thousand small-scale mines, including the one in which the workers were killed. Han Li's plan was to transport both nuclear weapons to this mine, drop them into this watery pit, and have the earth and water absorb the nuclear blasts.

Putting the plan into action, Chien An contacted the government agency responsible for coal mining and was told that the Urumqi mine was abandoned and still filled with water. That was the good news. The bad was that the area surrounding it was pockmarked with fissures so deep that an aircraft would likely rip off its landing gear if it tried to land. He also cautioned that the mine had produced bituminous coal, and a by-product was firedamp, a mixture of gases known to cause underground explosions. As of one year ago, when the mine was last checked, firedamp could still be detected. Chien An next checked to see if a heavy-lift helicopter, one capable of transporting each of the weapons and a forklift, was available. However, the nearest one capable of performing this task turned out to be several hundred miles from Urumqi. That left only one option—transporting the nuclear weapons by truck. Unfortunately, doing this would consume more than half the anticipated time till the expected detonation.

Once it was decided to transport the weapons by truck, Yan He walked out of the hangar and ordered the Class 6 NCO in charge of the guards to take whomever he needed and commandeer a forklift and a truck capable of carrying a two-ton load plus the weight of the forklift. The lieutenant colonel gave the NCO ten minutes.

Almost exactly ten minutes later, the NCO drove a black forty-ton Sinotruk into the hangar, whose large doors had been opened. The twelve-wheeled truck, which weighed fifteen tons and was thirty-nine feet long, eight feet wide, and thirteen feet high, had been commandeered from the next hangar. In the back was a forklift.

Once the NCO and the two guards with him had vacated the vehicle, Yan He quickly occupied the driver's seat and directed Cancelliere to sit next to him. Moretti, who knew how to operate a forklift from a summer job with a construction company in Anchorage, quickly stacked one crate on the other and transported them up the steel ramps and into the rear of the vehicle. As he was doing this, Han Li grabbed half a dozen flashlights and various tools from the aircraft hangar, in the event they were needed, and threw them into the back of the Sinotruk. She then sat behind the wheel of the van that the guards used for transport and started the engine. After the forklift and crates were secured, Moretti and Bonaquist joined her.

The Urumqi airport was ten miles from the mine. That wasn't a great distance and should have been a ten-minute drive, except that the road leading to the mine was as pockmarked with fissures as the ground surrounding it. Avoiding these rips in the earth kept both vehicles' speed to that of crosstown traffic in Manhattan.

Geologists referred to what they were heading to as a slope mine, one that inclined downward until it reached the coal seam. By the time the Nemesis team reached it, Moretti calculated that they had approximately twenty-five to thirty minutes before the weapons detonated—assuming his and Han Li's estimate was correct. For all they knew, the weapons could go off at any second.

Moretti backed the forklift off the Sinotruk, and as everyone watched, he pushed the accelerator pedal to the floor and headed for the mine's entrance. As he passed the van, Han Li leaped aboard and climbed onto the top crate.

"I'll direct you," Han Li said as she removed the flashlight from under her belt. Moretti also had taken one when he went into the bed of the Sinotruk, but he kept it in the small of his back.

Not far from the entrance, Han Li yelled for Moretti to stop. It was too late. The forklift hit the swirling ring of water in front of them at full speed. The crates entered the vortex, followed by the forklift. Upon hitting the ink-black water, Moretti and Han Li were immediately pulled under by a strong undercurrent and dragged and bounced along tunnel walls. Fifteen seconds later, they surfaced in a small chamber, which had some air but, by the smell of it and the work their bodies needed to get it into their lungs, not much. Neither showed ill effects, other than numerous scrapes and bruises.

"Any idea where we are?" Han Li asked, still holding her flashlight and shining it toward Moretti.

"None. All I know is that we changed direction underwater twice, and I left some skin on the tunnel walls until the current spit us in here, which is probably a side tunnel."

"I can hold my breath for quite a while. That said, I don't think we'll be able to swim against this current and find our way out before we run out of air."

"Agreed," Moretti said. "Not that it matters. If our estimate is anywhere near correct, twin nuclear explosions will vaporize us, this water, and a big chunk of this mine before long."

"Then I guess we'd better come up with plan B."

"Do we have one?"

"I'm working on it."

When Moretti and Han Li didn't return within ten minutes, Yan He got into the driver's seat of the van and, with Bonaquist and Cancelliere sitting beside him, turned the headlights on high and started down the entry ramp to the mine. They hadn't gone far when Yan He saw the swirling water in front of him and slammed on the brakes. Thankfully, the van was light and had good brakes. Even so, they slid to a stop only two feet from the water. No one needed to state the obvious—that Moretti and Han Li hadn't been as lucky. There was only one way in and out of the mine. If they weren't here, then they'd driven the forklift and crates into the swirling vortex in front of them and were now at the bottom of the mine shaft.

After a moment of silence, Yan He said, "Let's go. There's nothing we can do for them, and we need to leave before these weapons detonate."

Cancelliere and Bonaquist solemnly nodded their agreement.

CHAPTER 17

MORETTI AND HAN Li shone their lights around the chamber, looking for a way out.

"We're able to breathe," said Moretti, "which means that some air is getting in, although not much. If we find where it's coming from, there might be an opening for us to get out of here. You take this side of the chamber, and I'll inspect the other."

Han Li agreed.

Moretti swam fifteen feet to the other side of the chamber and pointed his flashlight above his head to begin his search. Almost immediately, he noticed a thick layer of slime covering a one-inch protrusion from the tunnel ceiling. Moretti had an idea of what it was and wanted to verify his hunch. Unfortunately, it was five feet beyond his reach. When he told Han Li what he'd discovered, she swam over to help.

"Climb onto my shoulders and see what's up there," Moretti said as she glided to his side.

With his help, Han Li lifted herself out of the water and onto his shoulders. At five foot eleven, she was easily able to inspect what Moretti had spotted, and after wiping away the slime with the forearm of her shirt, she confirmed that it was a four-by-four-foot steel grate.

As Moretti held onto the chamber wall with one hand and kept his light focused on the grate with the other, Han Li tugged at the release mechanism and, after a brief struggle, got the metal lever to move. Once the lever was in the full up position, the grate dropped toward her. Shining her light into the interior of what now appeared to be a ventilation shaft, she saw a steel rung ladder running along the interior and told Moretti what she'd found.

"This is probably an intake or a return airway," Moretti said. "Is there a fan at the top?"

Han Li pointed her flashlight above her. "No."

"There'll be ventilation shafts throughout the mine—some push air in, some suck it out. The owner of the mine probably removed and sold the fans when the mine closed. Given the rungs in the shaft, it seems to have doubled as an escape tunnel. There's probably an extension ladder on the floor of the mine to get to the grate. But good luck finding that, even if it wasn't also sold."

Han Li grabbed hold of the bottom rung of the airway ladder, letting her body extend down toward Moretti. "Climb up," she said.

With his flashlight wedged in his belt and pointed upward, Moretti grabbed Han Li's legs and saw the look of anguish on her face as he hefted his 230 pounds up her body. Trying to take as much weight off her as he could, he put his feet against the mine wall as he climbed. Just as he reached her waist and was stretching to grab the rung above her hands, Han Li's fingers spasmed, and she involuntarily released her grip.

What happened next was a matter of rapid reflex rather than forethought. At the same instant he felt her body begin to drop, he pushed off the mine wall and grabbed the lower rung of the ventilation shaft ladder with his left hand and

Han Li's right arm with the other. He then pulled her up high enough so that she could grab onto his rung.

It took only a few minutes to climb to the top of the ventilation shaft, where Han Li lifted the red emergency release lever and threw open the five-foot-square grate. She and Moretti could see the Sinotruk next to the mine's entrance a hundred yards away, but the van was gone. Neither had to tell the other that they were beyond their back-of-the-envelope calculation as to when the detonations would occur. The expressions on their faces conveyed the extreme urgency of the moment: they had to get the hell out of Dodge. Both ran as fast as they could to the vehicle, with Moretti getting into the driver's seat and Han Li jumping in next to him. The key was still in the ignition, and after bringing the truck to life, Moretti began weaving his way around the fissures as he headed toward Urumqi. However, the Sinotruk was a fifteen-ton beast and as nimble as an elephant in a forest. They weren't going anywhere quickly.

"There's a possibility these weapons never had their timers activated," Han Li said, cinching her seat belt and shoulder harness as tight as she could.

"Do you believe that?" Moretti asked, continuing to swerve the tanklike vehicle around fissures, some of which were over ten feet wide and thirty to forty feet deep. His voice was much louder than normal and had the edginess of urgency to it, reflecting the seriousness of the situation they were in.

"Not with this level of planning. This group wouldn't have left anything to chance," Han Li answered, raising her voice to be heard over the deep grinding sound the Sinotruk made as Moretti shifted gears.

"We may have the timing wrong, but not what's going to happen."

"What's a safe distance from an underground nuclear explosion?" Han Li asked.

"Remembering my military training, generally three to five miles. However, we're dealing with two nuclear devices. We need to be a hell of a lot farther than the third of a mile or so that we've traveled."

One and a quarter seconds later, both weapons detonated.

When the explosion occurred, Yan He, Cancelliere, and Bonaquist were two and a half miles from the twin detonations. That was an insignificant distance considering that the resulting shockwave traveled at two thousand miles per hour and had little chance to dissipate before it passed below the van. The ground beneath the vehicle undulated so violently that the van was thrown into the air and flipped onto its left side.

Once the undulations subsided, Yan He, Cancelliere, and Bonaquist exited the vehicle through one of the broken windows. Looking back toward the entrance to the mine, all they could see was a massive crater. Taking out their cell phones, each tried to place a call for help, but none of the phones worked. The EMP pulse had destroyed the circuitry inside the phones and rendered them useless.

Four hours after the nuclear explosions, a Z-20 helicopter flew over the van and landed fifty yards away. Yan He, Bonaquist, and Cancelliere, who'd waved to the aircraft from the moment they saw it on the horizon, got on board. After they told the pilot that no one else was coming, the helicopter took off and, at Yan He's direction, flew over the crater. The enormous hole that now occupied the space where the mine had once stood was, as best they could determine, half a mile deep and at least that distance wide. As Yan He solemnly told the pilot to head back to the airport, an expression of deep sadness covered each passenger's face; they knew Moretti and Han Li were dead.

It was dark and cold a hundred feet below what had once been the old mining road. Wedged between two enormous wedges of coal, the giant Sinotruk was pointing into a fissure over two thousand feet deep. Moretti and Han Li, still strapped to their seats, didn't yet realize their situation because each was unconscious.

Moretti opened his eyes twenty minutes after the explosion. Not able to see because of the enveloping darkness, and with the right side of his forehead throbbing, he pulled the flashlight from under his belt and turned it on. Touching the source of his pain, he came away with blood on his hand. Putting his fingers to his head again, he felt a six-inch gash that began just over his ear. Since the blood seemed to be clotting, he believed that the wound was superficial.

Pointing the flashlight to his right, he saw that Han Li was hanging motionless in her seat, restrained only by her harness. Running the light over her body, Moretti didn't see any blood on her face or clothing, but he did notice a large knot in the center of her forehead. The fact that she was unconscious worried him. However, what concerned him more was her erratic breathing. He released his harness and stood in the area around the brake and gas pedals, which was now the floorboard of the vehicle. He then slowly released Han Li from her seat belt and gently laid her at his feet so that she was lying flat. In a sedan or SUV, this area was small; in a Sinotruk it wasn't. He'd just knelt and inspected her airway, to make sure that it was unobstructed, when the truck shook. It wasn't a violent shake—more a tremor. However, when he pointed his light at the large coal outcroppings that were keeping the truck from plummeting into the chasm, it was clear to him that a vehicle weighing fifteen tons would eventually work its way free. He couldn't be certain when that would be, but with the aftershocks likely to continue, it probably wouldn't be long.

Moretti glanced at his watch out of habit, but it had been rendered useless by the EMP. Looking at the sky, which was rapidly transitioning to darkness, he knew that it would be too dangerous to try to climb out of the crater now and get help. He'd need to wait until daylight, if he could—the truck shook again but this time moved downward a foot before the outcroppings again prevented it from going further. Time was running out.

"This rust bucket was all that was available?" Cancelliere asked as he hoisted himself into the aging Chinese Z-11 six-seat training helicopter.

"You're beginning to sound like Moretti," Bonaquist replied as he strapped himself in. "This is it. The Z-20 doesn't have a searchlight, and this does. We're lucky it was here."

"You're right," Cancelliere conceded, tightening his safety straps and looking down at the corroding floor plates beneath his feet. "I think."

"We all agreed that we need to look for Moretti and Han Li, if for no other reason than to recover their bodies," Yan He said.

"Assuming they weren't vaporized or that we can see what's left of them in a crater that looks to be over twenty football fields from end to end," Cancelliere added.

"Whether we find them or not, we'll at least get closure," Bonaquist said.

"I never should have allowed Han Li to get onto the forklift," Yan He said. "It should have been me."

Cancelliere and Bonaquist looked at each other with piqued interest. It wasn't so much what Yan He had said but how he had said it.

"Were you and Han Li an item?" Cancelliere asked.

The helicopter lifted off and headed toward the crater.

"I was friends with her uncle, Cho Ling, for more than a decade before his death earlier this year. During that time there were many occasions when I saw and spoke with her. As you Americans would say, I admired her from afar. I didn't have the courage to pursue my admiration any further."

"Did she know how you feel?" Bonaquist asked.

"I don't believe so. There's no reason why she should. Now there's one last thing I can do to honor her—recover her body and return it to Beijing, where her greatness can be acknowledged."

When they arrived at the crater, Yan He told Cancelliere and Bonaquist to fasten a lifeline belt around their waists, after which he slid open the pilot-side door of the helicopter. "These belts will keep us from falling out," he said, pointing to his belt and the steel cable connecting it to a metal ring inside the helicopter, "since we'll have to lean out the side door in order to look for her below."

"Them," Bonaquist said.

Yan He nodded, acknowledging that they were searching for Moretti too, but it was clear that for him this was all about finding Han Li. He then walked up front and instructed the pilot to begin his grid pattern across the crater.

Moretti heard the Z-11 long before it reached the crater. Releasing his harness, which he earlier had fastened himself back into, he poked his torso out the driver's window, pointed his flashlight to the sky, and started waving his arms as the sound drew near. But the helicopter passed directly overhead, its view of the Sinotruk obstructed by the towers of coal surrounding the vehicle. As the helicopter passed, Moretti was able to see, thanks to the powerful light shining into the chasm, that he was about 125 feet below the surface. As an Army Ranger, he had been on more than his fair share of search and rescue missions. Therefore, he knew that the pilot was probably flying a standard grid pattern that would ensure no area of the crater was left unsearched. The fact that the aircraft was now past him meant that the pilot wouldn't be flying overhead again.

Turning his attention to Han Li, Moretti saw that her breathing was growing increasingly labored. As he knelt beside her, the tip of the pencil that he'd earlier picked up and put into his pants pocket dug into his thigh. The pain from the skin prick wasn't great, but the string of disappointments he'd suffered was, and he let out a string of curses as he grabbed the offending pencil, preparing to fling it into the abyss. That's when he remembered something that he'd learned in Ranger training. A plan began to formulate. On the plus side, it would enhance their chance of discovery. On the negative, it would start a chain of events that would kill them if the helicopter didn't come back.

As it turned out, the fifteen-ton Sinotruk had gouged a ledge five feet long, three feet wide, and six feet deep in one of the coal outcroppings before coming to an abrupt stop. Moretti knew it was the perfect place to put Han Li since the truck would eventually work its way free of the outcroppings. After she was safe, he'd retrieve the pair of orange jumper cables he'd seen tangled in the torn canvas that had once covered the rear cargo area. With the cables and the pencil, what he had in mind would absolutely get someone's attention.

With his flashlight wedged under his belt and pointing at the ledge, he reached down and picked up Han Li. He then stepped through the shattered passenger window and onto the ledge. After gently laying her down, he wadded his jacket and placed it under her head, tilting it back as he did so that she would have an easier time breathing.

Once Han Li was settled, he climbed into the cargo compartment, untangled the cables from the canvas, and placed them around his neck. The entire process took less than thirty seconds. However, as he was about to step back onto the ledge, a severe aftershock erupted, almost catapulting him into the abyss. Instinctively grabbing on to the steel support rib adjacent to him, he held on with both hands as the vehicle plunged five feet before coming to a jolting stop. Chunks of coal, some big enough to crush his head, streaked past him and slammed into the rear of the cargo compartment.

Moretti pulled his flashlight from under his belt, pointed it toward Han Li, and saw that the overhang above the ledge had protected her from the falling debris. Relieved, he worked his way down the right side of the vehicle. The Sinotruk's hood had been ripped off during its initial plunge, so the engine was exposed. Moretti easily found the battery, connected the orange jumper cables to its terminals, took a deep breath, and moved on to his next step.

CHAPTER 18

THE SINOTRUK'S TWO diesel tanks were between the driver's cab and the cargo bed. Moretti went to the passenger-side tank, removed the fuel cap, and then took the pencil from his pocket. He attached a jumper cable lead to each end of the pencil, which began to smolder and eventually burn. He then laid the ignited pencil across the opening to the diesel tank and started climbing up the side of the truck toward the ledge holding Han Li.

Moretti had learned in Ranger training that diesel fuel was inherently hard to ignite. Conversely, its vapor was highly combustible. Therefore, a burning pencil would eventually set off the vapor rising from the fuel tank. The resulting explosion would consume the vehicle in a fire that, hopefully, would be visible for some distance. Han Li should be protected from the conflagration because of the truck's five-foot drop during the aftershock, putting it below her now. The blast would go upward, past Han Li's protected position on the ledge, and be large enough for the helicopter passing overhead to notice. At least, that was the plan.

When the diesel vapor ignited, Moretti was on his way to Han Li. The resulting flame was everything he'd expected and more, towering high above the outcrops. Although the explosion was much more violent than he'd anticipated, he was unharmed except for some singed hair and eyebrows. Han Li survived unscathed. As positive as this was, the negative side of his plan was now on display. They were surrounded by a combustible fuel that he'd just ignited, and the coal around them was starting to burn. If the helicopter didn't find them, they'd soon be in the center of hell.

Yan He looked down into the canyons and gullies of broken coal and saw nothing but a deformed landscape of coal that went deeper than he'd anticipated. There was no way anyone could have survived the explosion that had produced this, nor were they going to find Moretti and Han Li's bodies.

"I think it's time we leave," Yan He said to Cancelliere and Bonaquist, who both nodded in agreement after seeing the destructive aftermath of the twin nuclear explosions.

Yan He went forward and told the helicopter pilot to return to the Urumqi airport, after which the aircraft banked right. Two-thirds of the way into its turn, both men spotted a soaring flame in the distance. Yan He didn't have to tell the pilot what to do. The aircraft leveled out and quickly accelerated toward the site of the flame. Soon the Z-11 was hovering over the Sinotruk, which was engulfed in fire. On the ledge above it were Moretti and Han Li.

"Do we have a rope or anything else we can lower to them?" Yan He asked the pilot.

"There's a twenty-foot piece of old twisted cotton rope in the corner, but I'm not sure it could hold the weight of even one person. We use it as a soft tie-down."

Yan He went to see. One look at the worn and frayed rope told him that it wasn't strong enough to hold anyone. He returned to the cockpit.

"You're right about the rope. Get this thing closer to them!" Yan He yelled to the pilot. "The flame's almost to their ledge."

The pilot took the aircraft down, but the thermals caused by the rising heat from the spreading coal fires rocked the aircraft from side to side, nearly pushing it into one of the jagged outcroppings. The pilot, who was a helicopter flight instructor in the PLA, was doing all he could to descend, maintain control, and keep the blades away from the jagged interior of the crater. But the closest he could get was twenty feet from the ledge.

Yan He, Bonaquist, and Cancelliere, who'd retreated from the open aircraft door when the Z-11 was being bounced around, held on tightly to their steel safety lines, which were fastened to the helicopter's floor strut by a locking rope clip.

Looking at the three lifelines and the clip, Bonaquist came up with an idea. "I think I know how we can reach Moretti and Han Li," he said, and he told them his idea.

"If this doesn't work, then the three of us will literally be the wick to the flame," Cancelliere replied. "But it's our only option."

Yan He agreed that they had no other choice.

While Bonaquist's steel safety line remained cinched around his waist and fastened to the helicopter's floor strut by the locking rope clip, Yan He removed his clip and attached it to the line around Bonaquist's waist. Cancelliere in turn attached his clip to Yan He's line, thereby creating a twenty-foot human chain whereby all three men were bound together, with Bonaquist anchored to the aircraft's floor strut. After all three men confirmed they were ready, Cancelliere lowered himself out of the helicopter, followed by Yan He. Bonaquist sat on the floor with his back against the steel aircraft passenger seats and his arms wrapped around the metal tubing underneath. He grunted from the enormous weight he was supporting, which pulled with a great deal of force at the lifeline around his waist.

The thermals were becoming worse as the fire continued to spread. The pilot was struggling to maintain his altitude and avoid the spires of coal surrounding him. Cancelliere, the lowest of the two men hanging outside the open cabin door, was trying his best to reach Moretti and Han Li, but he was getting raked by the flames coming from the truck.

"We need to get lower and create a pendulum motion," Cancelliere yelled to Yan He, who shook his head, indicating that he didn't understand. "We need Bonaquist to get closer to the door and swing us back and forth," he clarified.

Yan He nodded that he understood and relayed what was needed to Bonaquist, who let go of the seat supports and moved toward the helicopter door. Bonaquist looked at his rope clip before he joined Yan He and Cancelliere, questioning whether the floor strut was strong enough to support the weight of three men. He nevertheless lowered himself outside the aircraft, thereby adding another ten feet to the human chain they'd formed. In a matter of seconds, everyone began to rock the cable back and forth, sending Cancelliere in and out of the truck's flames, but closer to the ledge with every swing.

Moretti, who had been watching what was unfolding, seemed to understand what his friends were doing. He picked up Han Li, and as Cancelliere swung over the ledge, Moretti shoved her into the major's waiting arms. Seeing the handoff, the pilot backed away and lifted the three men and Han Li away from the ledge as Moretti watched, with the flames encroaching on him from all sides.

The Z-11 climbed out of the crater and gently lowered everyone to the ground.

"We need to go back and get Moretti," Yan He said to the pilot once the helicopter landed.

"There's a problem," Bonaquist said, joining Yan He while Cancelliere tended to Han Li. He pointed to the steel strut in the center of the helicopter, which was bent and all but separated from the floor of the aircraft.

"It's a wonder it didn't pop out while we were swinging back and forth," Yan He said. "We barely reached Han Li with our three lifelines fully extended. I don't think the struts under the seats, the only other alternative where we could attach the rope clip, are designed to take this type of weight. Even if they were, the four-plus feet we'd lose by attaching the lifeline there would mean we couldn't get low enough to rescue Moretti."

"You saw the fire," Cancelliere said, joining them. "He has minutes before he's engulfed in flames. Jack, you stay here and look after Han Li. I saw something while swinging toward Han Li, and I think I know how we can get Moretti out. But I'll need Yan He to interpret what I say to the pilot."

"Then let's go. We're wasting time," Yan He replied, getting into the helicopter.

A moment later, the Z-11 was airborne and streaking back to the crater.

With the fire literally lapping at his feet, Moretti had nowhere to go. As he placed his back flat against the wall of coal, he saw the helicopter's light racing toward him. Seconds later, it hovered about thirty feet away. Cancelliere poked his reddened face out the side door as Yan He crouched beside him. Cancelliere cupped his hands around his mouth and yelled something, but the ex-Ranger didn't quite believe what he'd heard. However, there was no mistaking what Cancelliere said next: "Just do it!" With the fire now brushing Moretti's pant legs, he was out of time. Looking down into the abyss, he bent his knees and leaped into the chasm.

Moretti managed to hit his target and, more importantly, not roll off the four-by-six-foot ledge he'd landed on. The ledge on which he'd been standing seconds ago not only was consumed in flames now but also had small gas explosions on it. These sent chunks of coal raining down onto his current ledge. Moretti didn't have to think too far back to recall that Chien An's mining expert had said that this mine had bituminous coal within it. What he was seeing were explosions from the gas within the coal. Sooner or later, some large chunks would be sent in his direction. If that didn't kill him, the fire working its way down to his ledge from above would. At best, he had five to ten minutes before that happened. However, this time there was nowhere else to go. There was no ledge below to which he could jump, and the helicopter, which had a rotor diameter of slightly over thirty-five feet, couldn't get closer than twenty because of the ragged spires of coal that were in front of him.

Fortunately, Cancelliere seemed to have worked something out because the next thing Moretti saw was the helicopter descending and hovering approximately thirty feet above him, about as close as it could get without its rotors hitting one of the coal spires, and a steel line extending toward him, which seemed to have been cobbled together from the lines previously worn by his teammates. However, even if he jumped and tried to grab it, the steel line was a couple of feet beyond his reach. That problem seemed to be solved when Cancelliere, wearing a pair of aviation gloves, slid down the lifeline and, upon reaching the end, extended his arm to Moretti.

"Ready to get out of here?" Cancelliere asked.

"I never want to see another mine. Let's go."

"Get a firm grip on the cable," he said, grabbing Moretti's forearm and helping him get to the lifeline. He untied a piece of fabric from around his waist—it appeared to be Yan He's shirt, torn in half. "Use this to tie onto the cable and then secure it to your wrists," Cancelliere instructed, handing Moretti the torn shirt.

Moretti did as he was told, looping the torn shirt twice around his right wrist and tying it to the lifeline. Once he was secure, Cancelliere gave a thumbs-up to Yan He, who told the pilot to pull them up. As the helicopter began to ascend, there was an enormous explosion from the fiery coal face adjacent to the helicopter, followed by two more explosions in rapid succession—each propelling numerous pieces of coal, from the size of a cannonball to that of a desk, in every direction. The outside of the helicopter was pummeled, but thankfully the debris didn't hit the blades. Moretti, who had a firm grip on the end of the rope, was struck by two cannonball-sized pieces; one hit him in the back, taking his breath away, and the other was a glancing blow off his left leg. Cancelliere wasn't as fortunate—a piece of coal the size of a portable copier hit him square in the chest. It killed the courageous rescuer instantly and propelled his body into the chasm. Moretti saw it happen and screamed as he watched the lifeless body of his friend, the person who'd just saved his life for a second time, plunge out of sight into the darkness below.

Moretti was lowered to the ground not far from Han Li, after which the Z-11 landed. When Bonaquist saw only Yan He and the pilot exit the aircraft, sorrow came over his face.

"Peter?" Bonaquist asked Moretti.

"Ripped off the rappel line after being hit by a large piece of coal. But he was probably dead on impact. He died saving me, Jack."

"He died doing his job. What we do is inherently dangerous—you know that. Six months ago, you were shot twice and had a knife embedded to its hilt in your back. You almost died."

"It's hard to accept that my friend is dead."

"For all of us."

"How's Han Li?" Moretti asked, changing the subject.

"Her breathing isn't getting any better. We need to get her to the hospital in Urumqi pronto."

It took thirty minutes for the Z-11 to reach the hospital in Urumqi, where Yan He's rank of lieutenant colonel got Han Li immediate attention from a raft of doctors and nurses. Moretti tried to enter the emergency room to see what was going on, only to get the door slammed in his face. He went back to the waiting room and took a seat next to Bonaquist while the hospital staff tried to save Han Li's life.

CHAPTER 19

THE DAY FOLLOWING the nuclear explosions, President Ballinger received a call from Vladimir Putin, and a deal was struck. In exchange for the United States keeping secret the pedigree of the nuclear weapons that had detonated in Urumqi, along with Russia's involvement, an envelope containing information that Ballinger would find extremely interesting would arrive at the White House shortly.

The envelope arrived thirty minutes after the call ended. After a multitude of tests for harmful agents and nanotechnology devices were performed, the envelope from the Russian embassy was taken to the Oval Office. When the president finished reading the contents within, he asked his administrative assistant, Mary Rinell, a former Marine Corps master sergeant, to get a message to Senator Lynn: "He needs to get his fat ass to the Oval Office now, whether he's sober or not."

"Yes, Mr. President," Rinell replied.

"And make sure to tell him that I'll have the Secret Service pick him up, so he can forget about giving me any lame excuses like he's needed in Congress."

Senator Rufus Lynn walked into the White House with the confidence of a prizefighter going into the ring while knowing the fix was in. Deducing that the president had gotten wind that Lynn had the security videos from Site R and the satellite photos from Beck, he believed that Ballinger now wanted to negotiate. In Washington, where there was enough backstabbing to make what had happened to Julius Caesar seem normal, everything was negotiable because no one gave away something for nothing. Therefore, he fully expected to make a deal with POTUS and then still release the information he'd received from Gorkin.

When he entered the Oval Office, the president was seated behind his desk and didn't bother to get up when he approached. Nor did Ballinger offer to shake his hand. Instead, unsmiling, he pointed to the chair in front of his desk. Lynn thought this unusual behavior for someone who wanted to horse-trade.

"Mr. President," Lynn said.

"Senator. I wanted to speak with you face-to-face because what I have to say affects our national security so greatly that I thought it should remain just between us."

Lynn gave a condescending smile. "I wholeheartedly agree, Mr. President."

"The matter I want to address is this," the president said, taking six photographs from the envelope on his desk and handing them to Lynn.

Lynn looked down at the photos. The first two showed Lynn meeting with Gorkin at the Capital Grille. In them the senator was giving the FSB major photographs of a Russian Skat as well as a photo showing members of the Nemesis team. From the angle, it appeared that the photos of Lynn had been taken from a camera hidden in the corner of his booth.

The expression on Lynn's face was one of resignation rather than surprise, as he realized that habitually using the same booth at the restaurant had opened him up to this type of surveillance. The next two photos were enlargements showing that what Lynn had shown Gorkin had "Top Secret" stamped at the top of it. The last two photos were of Lynn sitting with Gorkin in the Fireplace Hall at the Russian embassy.

Once Lynn was finished looking at the photographs, the president handed him two sets of stapled pages. "Those are the transcriptions of both your conversations with FSB major Yevgeny Gorkin."

Lynn's face had gone from alcoholic red to marshmallow white as he looked at what he'd been handed.

"I'm sure if I asked the attorney general, he'd say you should be charged with treason and made an example of. What do you think, Senator?"

Lynn was speechless. The president had him dead to rights.

"As I see it, you have two choices. One is that I have you arrested, so that your constituents see you on the evening news being perp-walked out of the White House. The other is that you resign from office and forgo any future involvement with politics, publishers, or news organizations—forever."

"What assurance do I have that the next person sitting in this office won't decide to prosecute me?"

"None. However, besides me, only Putin and Gorkin know about this. If you keep your word, your reprehensible actions will remain secret."

"And what about you, Mr. President?" Lynn asked. "This farce of an analytical unit at Site R is, in reality, a presidential hit squad hidden from congressional and judiciary oversight."

"In my role as commander in chief, black ops is technically under my purview and doesn't necessitate approval by either branch of government. My job is to maintain our nation's security by whatever means. And that group, which you incorrectly characterize as a hit squad and so freely exposed, protects this great nation. Therefore, let me add that our understanding also means that you'll never mention or imply that such a group exists. If someone should miraculously learn of their existence, our deal's off."

"What if someone else stumbles on them, just as I did?"

"Pray they don't. I expect your resignation to be announced on national TV before the end of the day. You're a piece of shit. Now get your fat ass out of my office."

The announcement, made on the steps of the US Capitol, was the lead story for every national news organization. Senator Rufus Lynn, his party's presumed presidential nominee for the upcoming presidential election, had resigned from Congress due to ill health. Although no one questioned that the overweight and alcoholic senator might be sick, his colleagues were nonetheless stunned. However, in the end they attributed his resignation to equal parts ill health and the knowledge that he couldn't defeat Ballinger in the upcoming election.

The surrounding fog gradually began to dissipate, revealing a familiar face. It was Moretti, sleeping in a chair beside her bed. Touching his hand, Han Li saw his eyes open and a look of relief appear on his face.

"How are you feeling?" he asked.

"A slight headache, and I'm thirsty, but otherwise not too bad."

Moretti went to the nightstand and poured a glass of water from the gray plastic pitcher. He brought the glass to her and supported it as she slowly drank.

"How long have I been unconscious?"

"Almost two days. The doctor said you have a concussion, but that you'd regain consciousness in your own time. Let me get him for you."

"Not yet," she said. "Help me sit up."

Moretti found the remote control for the bed and raised the back.

"How did I get here? The last thing I remember is our truck being hurled into the air."

"It's a long story. Are you sure you're up for hearing this now?"

"Tell me everything," she insisted.

Moretti spent the next twenty minutes giving her the details of what had happened, including their improbable escape and Cancelliere's death.

"I feel terrible about Peter's death," Han Li said.

"It should have been me—would have been had he not rappelled down and hauled my ass out of there."

"You made that same life-and-death decision about me, except the outcome wasn't the same."

Moretti looked at Han Li for a few moments, trying to build up the courage to say how he felt about her. Finally, he just let the words flow. "When you were unconscious, I looked within myself and thought about what my life would be like without you in it—and I didn't like what I saw."

Han Li gave him with a quizzical look.

"Don't get excited. I'm not proposing. What I'm saying is that I want to get to know you better. Let's take some time off and go someplace where no one's trying to kill us."

"And how do you propose we do that? Nemesis isn't a nine-to-five job where we can go away undisturbed while the world melts around us."

"I'll talk Cray into some R&R time. As banged up as we both are, he'll want to get us back in shape so we can once again be chased by those who want to kill us."

"Do you have a place in mind?"

"We'll decide that together."

"I'd love to go away with you," Han Li said, continuing to hold his hand tightly in hers.

Moretti had his back to the door, so he didn't see that Yan He had opened it. Yan He stared at Moretti holding Han Li's hand while she looked into his eyes. He had heard their conversation, and after hearing Han Li's answer, he quietly closed the door to the room.

CHAPTER 20

THE AIR ASTANA flight from Urumqi arrived at Moscow's Sheremetyevo International Airport at six in the evening. Kvachkov and his men were met by an FSB officer as they disembarked and were then escorted past customs and immigration. The four men were taken to a waiting car and driven fifteen miles southeast of the city, to the Zhukovsky International Airport, where they were put aboard an Ilyushin IL-76 cargo aircraft. The officer escorting them explained that they were being taken to their next assignment. Kvachkov had flown out of this airport many times before when Moscow wanted to keep the people or items it was transporting close to the vest. Exhausted, he and his men leaned back in their webbed seats, closed their eyes, and were soon fast asleep.

The flight was fourteen hours long. When the aircraft landed at its destination, Kvachkov looked out one of the small windows and immediately knew he was at the Sokol Airport in Magadan Oblast, Russia, because he'd been here several times in the past. Partially inside the Arctic Circle, it was the debarkation point for prisoners who were on their way to the country's most remote gulags. His two previous trips had been made to escort someone who could embarrass or harm the government or Vladimir Putin—which was apparently the category into which he and his men had just been placed.

The USS *Ohio*, SSGN-726, a two-football-field-long nuclear guided missile submarine, was on patrol in the Persian Gulf when its captain received a presidential directive to proceed to coordinates in the Arabian Sea, a distance of 1,481 miles. There it was to wait for the arrival of two unnamed passengers and follow the sealed orders within the courier pouch they carried.

An hour after the *Ohio* got to those coordinates and reported it was on station, a Sikorsky CH-53E Super Stallion helicopter lowered a man and a woman onto its deck. Once they were safely below and the submarine had resubmerged, the pair handed the captain the courier pouch. Within was a "captain's eyes only" order from the commander in chief. Upon reading it, the captain ordered his vessel to proceed at maximum speed to a spot three hundred miles off the coast of Pakistan. Once the *Ohio* was there, the captain summoned Moretti and Han Li to the bridge.

"This is the craft referenced in my orders," the captain said, looking through his periscope at the anchored 183-foot-long Benetti yacht named *The Golden One*. He then moved aside and gave Moretti and Han Li a view of the vessel before lowering the periscope. "My orders say to provide anything you request from this point forward. What do you want?"

Moretti told him.

The *Ohio* was repositioned two miles from the Benetti and remained submerged until two in the morning. At that time, it broke surface, and the crew brought out and inflated a seven-and-a-half-foot-long electric-motor rigid inflatable boat, or RIB in military parlance. They then lowered the RIB into the water and lashed it to the side of the sub. Moretti and Han Li, each wearing a wet suit, fin socks, and night-vision goggles, lowered themselves into the boat using a rope ladder. Each had a diver's knife fastened to the right leg and an HK416 assault rifle with suppressor slung over the shoulder.

They silently approached the yacht from the stern and tied the RIB to the swim platform. Photos from the drone had indicated that two guards were on duty every night—one on the top deck and the other on the deck that Moretti and Han Li were currently boarding. Neither guard seemed to patrol. Instead, they sat in comfortable deck chairs for most of their shift, leaving every hour or two for a stroll, a smoke, or to relieve themselves. Motion sensors and infrared camera alarms seemed to be either nonexistent or deactivated.

Moretti and Han Li were familiar with the layout of the Benetti thanks to the Nemesis tech team at Site R, which had been able to hack into the yacht builder's computer. Locating the vessel had taken slightly longer, but the navy could ultimately find and track almost anything at sea. In this case, once the Benetti's specs, the vessel's name, and other data had been entered into the navy's tracking system, a supercomputer had sorted through thousands of images until it found what it was looking for. In one of those images, Awalmir Afridi could be seen, surrounded by several naked women, in a hot tub on the main deck.

The United States had learned of the Benetti yacht from President Ballinger's conversation with the king of Saudi Arabia. Confronted with the fact that he'd called Putin, thereby effectively condoning—or at least setting off a chain of events that led to—Russia's intrusion into China, the king was anxious not to alienate either the Chinese or the Americans. The ruler of the House of Saud had given up

Al Hakim as a coconspirator in what had occurred and had provided US intelligence with a list of Al Hakim's assets. Then, in a joint effort to find Afridi, the Saudis had searched Al Hakim's residences while the United States looked for the yacht.

Moretti signaled for Han Li to take care of the guard on the upper deck, while he handled the one outside the entrance to the staterooms. The sea was calm and the night eerily quiet as Moretti approached the bow. There he saw the guard reclined in a lounge chair, smoking a cigarette. Moretti pulled his knife from its scabbard, stepped up behind his unsuspecting victim, and in one swift motion, placed his hand over the man's mouth and slit his throat. He'd just returned the knife to its scabbard when Han Li arrived.

Moretti opened the hatch that led to the staterooms, after which he and Han Li unslung their HK416 assault rifles and entered. Since the interior corridor was dimly lit, they didn't need their night-vision goggles and therefore raised them above their eyes. The passageway was covered from floor to ceiling with elegant wood that looked expensive and probably was, and the dim light came from four ornate crystal fixtures affixed to the bulkheads. There were four doors in the corridor—one on each side and a double set at the end. From the construction diagrams, they understood that the double doors led to the master stateroom.

When they reached the double doors, Moretti gently turned both of the handles, hoping that one would be unlocked. No such luck. Han Li then removed two lock picks from inside the sleeve of her wetsuit and, in less than a minute, unlocked one of the doors. Fortunately, the hinges were heavy and well maintained and made no noise as Han

Li slowly pushed the door open. Flipping down their night-vision goggles, the pair entered.

The master stateroom was slightly over five hundred square feet and was connected to a large bathroom on the deck below by an ornate spiral glass staircase. The room was dominated by a circular bed that rested on a foot-high platform. Behind it was a wall of windows over which thick drapes had been pulled, and on either side of the bed were wardrobe closets made from the same wood they'd seen in the passageway. In the center of the bed was their target—a pajama-clad Awalmir Afridi.

Han Li removed a strip of duct tape from the arm of her wet suit, bent over the terrorist, and roughly put it over his mouth. Immediately, Afridi awoke and tried to leap from his bed, only to receive Moretti's fist in his solar plexus. While their target was writhing in pain, Moretti flipped him onto his stomach and tightly bound his wrists and ankles with the duct tape that Han Li handed him. Once Afridi was fully trussed, the ex-Ranger placed a pillowcase over Afridi's head and lifted him across his shoulders in a fireman's carry.

"I'm tempted to trip and dump him into the water," Moretti said as they were making their way back to the RIB.

"It's tempting, but I believe we need to pick his brain."

"Yeah," Moretti replied, his tone indicating that he accepted that Afridi had to live but didn't like it. "Maybe I'll volunteer to waterboard this asshole."

After lowering their prisoner onto the RIB, they returned to the *Ohio*, where Afridi was taken to the brig and placed under 24/7 guard.

A week later, the *Ohio* resurfaced. Moretti and Han Li accompanied the zip-tied, hooded Afridi on deck and strapped him in a large metal basket that had been lowered from a hovering Chinese Navy Z-8 helicopter. The six-bladed transport had two very large, unsmiling Chinese military officers inside, and once the basket was level with the side door of the aircraft, one of them unstrapped Afridi and threw him onto the steel floor, after which the basket was brought on board and the door was closed.

The prisoner was then taken to a military airfield and flown to Mohe, the northernmost town in China, with only a river separating it from Siberia.

The prison commandant, Major Leung Tao, looked at the person before him and then at the papers he'd received by messenger from President Liu. Even though the man clearly wasn't Chinese, it didn't matter. The incarceration decree didn't provide a name, only a mandate that this person be imprisoned for life, the same sentence given to every other inmate. The only distinction with this prisoner was that he was to be separated from the others. The commandant interpreted this to mean that the man was to be placed in permanent solitary confinement.

Major Leung stepped close to Afridi, who was standing between two PLA officers, and looked him directly in the eyes. The terrorist returned a defiant look, the hatred apparent on his face. If not for the duct tape covering his mouth, there was a better than even chance that he'd have spit on his incarcerator. Unfazed by this hostility, Leung casually turned around and took a two-foot-long bamboo baton off his desk. With a practiced motion, he savagely jabbed the end of the baton into Afridi's midsection. As the terrorist grunted in pain and his knees buckled, the two officers holding his arms kept him from collapsing to the floor.

"Welcome to Mohe," Leung said in English, "the most remote and secure military prison in China. You are now prisoner number 41725. If you identify yourself by anything other than this number, you will be severely beaten. No one will ever know you're here or come to rescue you. That's because this facility doesn't officially exist. You'll remain here for the rest of your life. When you die, we'll throw you in the furnace with the rest of the garbage and erase all evidence from our books that there was ever a prisoner 41725. There's no escape, because there's nowhere for you to go. The nearest town is two hundred miles away, and you'd starve to death or be eaten by wolves or bears long before you got there. In the dead of winter, the outside temperature will be minus forty Fahrenheit, and our antiquated boilers can only heat the interior of our prison to at most fifty degrees. I have an additional heater to keep me warm. You won't."

Afridi's eyes began to widen. His sagging posture seemed to indicate that he now understood that he'd never again be free.

"You will be confined to your cell for all but one hour of the day, unless you're taken away for interrogation, which will occur frequently and generally without notice. If you cooperate, these sessions will be less painful than if you try to resist. If you lie or hide information from us, you'll be traumatized. You'll be in solitary confinement and allowed to shower once a week. If you are disruptive or disobey the guards, you'll be beaten, and your food will be taken away for one day. Do you understand?"

The prisoner nodded.

"A list of questions has been sent to me. To get started, I've selected one of these guards, whose brother was beheaded by one of your followers, to conduct your first interrogation."

Prisoner 41725 began to sweat despite the frigid temperature and rapidly looked to his left and right, not knowing which guard the commandant was referring to. A second later, the guard to his left released his grip and punched Afridi so hard in the ribs that a cracking sound could be heard.

"I don't believe an introduction to your interrogator will be needed." The commandant handed the guard the list he'd received. "Take him away, but make sure you don't kill him until I get the answers to these questions. After that, he's yours."

AUTHOR'S NOTES

This is a work of fiction. However, a substantial portion of *The Payback* accurately depicts historical events, places, and objects.

As represented, the dissolution of the Soviet Union did occur on December 26, 1991. The previous day, Mikhail Gorbachev, the eighth and last leader of the Union of Soviet Socialist Republics (USSR), resigned and was succeeded by Boris Yeltsin.

The Soviet Union did have 22,000 tactical nuclear weapons spread across four of its states—Kazakhstan, Belarus, Ukraine, and Chechnya. As the Soviet Union was disintegrating, the Ministry of Defense frantically tried to move these devices to sites rigidly controlled by Moscow. The Russians say that all nuclear weapons have been accounted for, but no one believes that. The Soviet Union was falling apart, and wages had not been paid to military and civilian workers for some time. As a result, there was a lower level of vigilance over tactical nuclear weapons in areas that were distant from Moscow. Also, as stated, inflation at this time was two thousand percent, corruption was rampant, and it is true that everything was for sale. A good article to read regarding this period is "Russia in Global Affairs" by Graham Allison, of the Belfer Center for Science and International

Affairs at the John F. Kennedy School of Government at Harvard, and Douglas Dillon, a professor of government at the Harvard Kennedy School.

The exile of Chechens by Stalin is accurately depicted. They were forcibly taken from their homes, placed onto cattle cars, and taken to Western Siberia in the middle of a particularly harsh winter. When they arrived, they were literally dumped in open fields and left to fend for themselves. It's been documented that half of the five hundred thousand who began that journey perished. A good account of this can be found in an article by Masha Gessen titled "Chechnya: What drives the separatists to commit such terrible outrages?" Therefore, the bad blood between the Chechens, who are predominately Sunni Muslims, and the Soviets/ Russians is accurately represented. Even though the land area of Chechnya is relatively small, somewhere between the sizes of Connecticut and New Jersey, the Chechens have been a generational headache for the Soviets and later the Russian government. Illustratively, in 1991, just as the Soviet Union was disintegrating, Chechen separatists declared their independence, believing they could get away with becoming an independent nation since Moscow had so many other problems. However, because of Chechnya's economic and strategic importance, the Kremlin wasn't about to let that happen. As a result, the conflict between them escalated into war, which continued until the Russians brutally squashed the rebellion and reestablished control.

The town of Miramshah exists and is in North Waziristan, Pakistan, approximately ten miles from the Afghanistan border. It continues to be the home of numerous terrorist groups and is often on the receiving end of CIA drone strikes.

The Pakistani government does denote good and bad militants, and the criteria for that determination are accurate. A January 31, 2015, *Newsweek* article by R. M. Schneiderman titled "Is Pakistan Really Cracking Down on Terrorism?" provides an excellent insight into the inter-dynamics of why Pakistan protects "good militants."

The Saudi royal family does have an estimated twenty-two thousand members, with approximately seven thousand designated as princes. That makes the ratio within the country one royal to one thousand nonroyals. However, only about two thousand royals possess real power and wealth. Royals do not receive salaries but are given government allowances, referred to as stipends, that are based on subjective factors. These payments can range anywhere from $800 to $270,000 per month. In total, these payments amount to an estimated $2 billion per year. The net worth of the entire royal family is said to be approximately $1.4 trillion, although no one will ever know for sure.

Arabic names can sometimes be confusing. In the case of Ahmed al-Khobar, the article "al" can mean "the" or "from." Sometimes you'll see it capitalized, and it may or may not be followed by a hyphen. Often it denotes the area where one's family is from. In this case, Ahmed al-Khobar means Ahmed from Khobar. One's name can also reference a character trait or profession. The name Husam Al Hakim, for example, translates into Husam the All-Wise. "Bin" translates into "son of." Therefore, Mahamat bin Salman is the son of Salman.

The Bacha Khan International Airport in Peshawar, Pakistan, is as portrayed. On May 1, 1960, Francis Gary Powers's U-2 did take off from there and was later shot down over the Soviet Union. As incredible as it sounds, the nine-thousand-foot runway is crossed by a rail line, but the latter is reportedly nonoperational—probably a good thing for passengers and aircrew alike.

My apologies to the Banque Saudi Fransi for portraying Husam Al Hakim as your depositor. In searching for a reputable financial institution whose name was a little out of the ordinary, I came across this bank, which is 31.1 percent owned by Credit Agricole, the second-largest bank in France, and ranks seventh among banks within Euroland. It therefore has both size and stature, something Al Hakim would have demanded of a financial institution.

Polonium-210 is an insidious and particularly lethal radioactive substance. As mentioned, it's 250,000 times more poisonous than hydrogen cyanide. The alpha particles it emits do not set off radiation detectors, nor can its gamma radiation be detected. Therefore, it's relatively easy to smuggle from country to country. The idea to use it in this book came from a story about Alexander Litvinenko, a former FSB agent who fled Russia and received political asylum in Great Britain. The Russians took exception to this change of loyalty and feared that more defectors would follow. Therefore, they wanted to make a public example of him. They accomplished their goal in spades, poisoning him with polonium-210. However, death from this substance is not immediate. After he became ill, it took several weeks for Litvinenko to die. For the sake of the story line, I sped up the death for all who encountered polonium-210. I do not know whether Caspian State University of Technology and Engineering in Aqtau has an alpha or gamma spectrometer.

The Mabahith, or Saudi secret police, is accurately described. Its agents operate with impunity and use torture, waterboarding, beatings, and other forms of abuse in their interrogations. They operate within the Ulaysha Prison in

Riyadh, which is where those arrested by the Saudi secret police are generally taken.

The one-time pad, or OTP, that Afridi and Al Hakim used to communicate with one another exists and is as described. An OTP is unbreakable so long as the key is random and not reused.

In describing King Turki bin Abdulaziz Al Saud's palace, I used a composite of the three Saudi Arabian residences owned by Prince Al-Waleed bin Talal. His Kingdom Palace contains three lakes, which are integrated with magnificent gardens. The Promotion Palace is a $300 million sand-colored residence with a mosque adjoining it. Although it's the smallest of the palaces in terms of land size, this sprawling residence has 317 rooms adorned with fifteen hundred tons of Italian marble, silk oriental rugs, gold-plated faucets, and 250 TV sets. It also contains five kitchens, one just for making desserts. The Oasis Palace, the largest of Al-Waleed's three residences, has a 700,000-square-foot lake, a private zoo, and other "essentials" of life.

The descriptions of the Azerbaijan, Aqtau, and Kazakhstan border crossings are fictional, invented for the sake of the story line to place adversity and stress in the path of Samara and his men.

Although the Yining Drilling Supply Company is fictional, the Diamec U8 drill is real. I chose this drill rig because it's heavy and replacing these drills with the nuclear weapons would obfuscate what was being transported in the crates. However, I modified the dimensions and weight of the drill for the sake of the story line.

Daheyanzhen exists, but the descriptions of the town and its sources of revenue were contrived by the writer for the sake of the story line.

The Russian embassy in Washington, DC, is situated on Mount Alto, the third-largest hill in Washington, DC, occupying the former site of a Veterans Administration hospital. As indicated, it commands a magnificent view of the White House, Pentagon, and State Department, giving the diplomats within the ability to conduct visual and electronic line-of-sight surveillance.

The National Reconnaissance Office does design, build, and operate all spy satellites for the United States government. Also, as represented, there is a huge NSA listening post at Fort Gordon, known as NSA/CSS Georgia. Residing there are intercept operators, linguists, and analysts who go through the enormous amount of signal intelligence relayed to the site via satellite. The exact speed of the NSA's computers is unknown, but it's generally acknowledged that they can perform one quadrillion operations per second, or a petaflop. Most believe, however, that those capabilities have grown to an exaflop—a staggering quintillion, or billion billion, operations per second.

The information on the Raven Rock Military Complex and Site R is accurate. It's considered to be the alternate Pentagon and quite possibly one of the alternate locations for the White House. In 2015 the DOD Base Structure Report described Raven Rock as encompassing 716 acres and containing sixty-eight buildings with a total usable space of 636,261 square feet.

Saudi Arabia does have several series of orbital communications satellites—the Arabsat, the SaudiComsat, and the SaudiGeoSat. All three are accurately described. The Arabsat-6A and the SaudiGeoSat both were built by Lockheed Martin and provide television, internet, telephone, and secure communications to customers in the Middle East,

Africa, and Europe. The SaudiComsat satellites are low-orbit microcommunications satellites, weighing about twenty-five pounds each, used to store and forward commercial communications. It's not known whether the US government has the plans to these satellites since their use is benign. However, for the sake of the story line, I assumed it does.

My thanks to Kimberly Amadeo for her August 21, 2018, article in *The Balance*: "US Trade Deficit with China and Why It's So High." The information presented in this article was used to illustrate the impact an economic crisis in China would have on the United States. Other data was obtained online from the Office of the United States Trade Representative, under a section designated as "US-China Trade Facts."

The process of decay within nuclear warheads and the maintenance required to keep them operational are as described. An excellent article by Allison Bond of New York University titled "Scienceline," in the April 15, 2009, issue of *Popular Science*, describes the aging of nuclear warheads.

The information presented regarding the handling of nuclear material is also accurate. According to physicist Dr. Gregory Greenman and other notable members of the science community, weapons-grade nuclear material such as plutonium-239 and uranium-235 can be handled by hand without any ill effects. This is because the alpha particles they emit lose their energy very quickly and therefore cannot even penetrate the epidermis layer of human skin.

Muons exist and are accurately described. The method of detecting hidden nuclear weapons using muons is still, as far as I know, being tested.

As described, nuclear bomb debris does hold clues as to who planted the bomb. For further information, please read a fascinating article by David Shiga in the November 8, 2010, issue of *New Scientist*.

Russian president Vladimir Putin commutes between his official residence in Novo-Ogaryovo and the Kremlin in a Russian-made Mi-8 helicopter. He previously made this commute by motorcade. However, growing public criticism of massive traffic jams caused by blocked roads and the cavalcade of vehicles accompanying him necessitated a change in transport. The offices for the president of the Russian Federation and his staff are in the Kremlin's old Senate building, which was built between 1776 and 1787 to house the Governing Senate of Imperial Russia. This structure is shaped like an isosceles triangle, a little over 330 feet to a side. It's adjacent to the Kremlin Wall on Red Square.

Manora is, as described, a small peninsula south of the Port of Karachi on the Arabian Sea, connected to the mainland by a seven-and-a-half-mile causeway called the Sandspit. I placed the marina there for the sake of the story line, to give Awalmir Afridi a plausible place to board Al Hakim's yacht and escape undetected.

The flying parameters of the Russian Skat drone are, according to publicly available information, accurate except for the craft's range, which is known only to the Russian military. It's unknown whether this drone is currently flying, but rumors are that it is and that it closely resembles Boeing's Phantom Ray in both design and performance characteristics. The Skat is thought to be an offensive drone whose mission is to attack air defense systems and marine targets with air-to-surface missiles. It's not thought to carry air-to-air missiles, nor does it appear to have advanced reconnaissance capabilities as depicted for the sake of the story line.

Khotilovo exists and is a military airfield north of Moscow that houses the MIG-31BM, a long-range interceptor fighter. It does not act as a command and control base for drones.

The Chinese train routes and stations described in the book are a product of my imagination, used to enhance the story line. However, the Y-30 transport and Z-20 helicopters are accurately described. Respectively, they are strikingly like America's C-130 and the UH-60 Black Hawk.

The role of Saudi Arabia in providing money to terrorist groups is well documented. In a December 2009 paper released by WikiLeaks, former secretary of state Hillary Clinton indicated that the kingdom was the world's largest source of funding for Islamist militant groups. She also said that "more needs to be done since Saudi Arabia remains a critical financial support base for al-Qaida, the Taliban, LeT and other terrorist groups." Within Saudi Arabia, militants soliciting funds often come into the country posing as holy pilgrims. They then set up front companies that are supposedly government-sanctioned charities, but in reality are established to launder money. This enables them to hide their monetary support for terrorist groups while at the same time receiving money from their benefactors under the guise of contributions to charity. There are many Arab charities that perform good work and have no association with terrorists. However, it's the rotten apple in the barrel that gets noticed and ends up tarnishing everyone. In addition to Saudi Arabia, the nations of Qatar, Kuwait, and the United Arab Emirates are also significant sources of militant money.

China is, as indicated, an enormous source of potential revenue for Russia. In May 2014, after meetings in Shanghai, Vladimir Putin and Chinese president Xi Jinping signed an agreement whereby China agreed to purchase natural gas from the Russian Federation over a thirty-year period. The value of that contract is estimated to be $400 billion. Earlier, President Xi had agreed to purchase $85 billion of oil from Russia. With almost half a trillion dollars of potential sales, Vladimir Putin has every reason to keep China happy.

The mining accident in Urumqi did occur. In October 2014 sixteen workers died when the tunnel they were working in collapsed. It's unknown whether that mine remains closed. However, after this incident the Chinese government shut down over two thousand small-scale coal mines because of concerns about their safety. There was no flooding in the Urumqi mine, at least as far I know. In addition, the interior and exterior descriptions of this mine and the surrounding area were changed for the sake of the story line.

Unlike electronic circuitry, a normal car battery is not affected by an EMP from a nuclear detonation. I got the idea of using jumper cables to ignite a wooden pencil from a July 8, 2012, article by David Galloway in *Lifehacker*. However, in his article Galloway cut notches into the side of the pencil, attached the jumper cable clips to it, then started the vehicle to get his flame. I took some liberties with this process because I wasn't sure that it was reasonable to assume that the Sinotruk's engine still would work.

Some may wonder why Moretti didn't blow himself up when he put the pencil above the fuel tank. That almost certainly would have happened if the truck ran on gasoline. However, diesel fuel is a combustible with an octane rating of 20–25, whereas gas is flammable liquid with an octane rating of 80–100. Therefore, unlike gasoline, diesel needs a high temperature and pressure ratio to burn. It also burns more easily in an atomized state, which is why I used vapor rising from the fuel tank to create combustion.

I took some liberties with the rigid inflatable boat, or RIB, that transported Moretti and Han Li from the USS *Ohio* to the Benetti yacht. In doing so I placed an electric motor on the RIB, in deference to its standard large-engine configuration, which allows it to attain speeds of forty to seventy knots, depending on size and weight. My apologies to the US Navy for tinkering with the inflation procedures and the configuration of the RIB.

Also, my apologies to the Benetti company for indicating that someone breached your computer system and for falling short of accurately describing the magnificent features and interior designs of your yachts.

Mohe is the northernmost town in China. Located fifty miles from the Russian border, it's the Chinese equivalent of Siberia. I was there in February, when the temperature can get to minus forty Fahrenheit. In fact, the temperature normally stays below freezing for seven months of the year, and the area experiences only ninety days when the climate is frost-free. While driving from the airport to the town of Mohe, I saw a prison a half mile from the road—or at least it looked like a place of incarceration. The compound contained several buildings, at least from what I could see, and was surrounded by high walls, razor wire, and guard towers. Curious, I asked my Chinese driver what this place was, but he refused to say, and we quickly encountered a language problem, wherein he said that he didn't understand my question. However, since Mohe is the northernmost town in China and a pencil point from Siberia, locating a prison there would make sense.

I believed that killing Awalmir Afridi, given that he was an extremist with no regard for human life, who was willing to kill millions to get his payback, would have been too kind a fate for someone this evil. Therefore, since Afridi was accustomed to the hot weather of the Middle East, I believed he'd have a hellish time spending the rest of his days in the frigid confines of Mohe and being interrogated by someone who had an obvious dislike for him.

ACKNOWLEDGMENTS

My continued thanks to an extraordinary group of friends who continue to unselfishly give me the benefit of their opinions and thoughts. They've been my guides when it's been difficult to see the forest for the trees.

To Kerry Refkin for providing invaluable recommendations on my story line. Your insights and perceptions continue to be extraordinary.

To the group—Scott Cray, Dr. Charles and Aprille Pappas, Doug Ballinger, Alexandra Parra, Ed Houck, Cheryl Rinell, Mark Iwinski, Mike Calbot, and Dr. Meir Daller—thank you for continuing to be my sounding boards.

To Zhang Jingjie for her research. No one is better at finding that needle in the haystack.

To Dr. Kevin Hunter and Rob Durst for making the incomprehensible comprehensible. Your cybersecurity skills are unparalleled.

To Clay Parker, Jim Bonaquist, and Greg Urbancic for the extraordinary legal advice you continue to provide.

To Bill Wiltshire and Debbie Layport for your superb financial and accounting skills.

To Zoran Avramoski, Piotr Cretu, Neti Gaxholli, Aleksandar Toporovski, and Billy DeArmond for your insights.

To Doug and Winnie Ballinger and Scott and Betty Cray: somehow the words "thank you" seem inadequate for the positive impact you've both made on the lives of so many who were unable to help themselves.

ABOUT THE AUTHOR

Alan Refkin is the author of five previous works of fiction and the coauthor of four business books on China. He received the Editor's Choice Award for *The Wild, Wild East* and for *Piercing the Great Wall of Corporate China.* The author and his wife, Kerry, live in southwest Florida, where he is currently working on his next Matt Moretti-Han Li novel. More information on the author, including his blog, can be obtained at alanrefkin.com.

Printed in the United States
By Bookmasters